THE ISLAND'S LIGHT

~ Dedication ~

To my cousin, Wade. May your Light never stop shining from above...
~ * ~

A special thank you to my long-time friend, Karen Jean, for helping make this dream of mine a reality...

~ * ~

TABLE OF CONTENTS

~ * ~

CHAPTER ONE ~ The Importance of Family

"Dad, hurry up, or we're going to miss our flight!" Elizabeth's exasperated voice could be heard as she hollered over her shoulder to her father.

Mitchell grunted as he tried in vain to move as fast as he could. Pushing a rolling cart with multiple layers of luggage was no easy task! The trip from the domestic arrival gate seemed a million miles from the pending departure building as he stopped to wipe the beads of sweat from his forehead.

The trio's arrival in Los Angeles had been delayed by an unexpected storm as they prepared for the flight out of North Carolina earlier that morning.

"Well, perhaps if *some people* didn't feel the need to pack up and travel with the entire contents of their closet, I could move a little faster!" Mitchell grumbled under his breath.

"I acknowledge your frustration, and I sympathize with your pain, Mitchell." Eloise shot back with a sarcastic retort. "What did you expect? That I would travel *all the way* to Hawaii with just a carry-on? Silly man, you know me better than that!"

Eloise gave Elizabeth a wink as she lifted her dark sunglasses to give Mitchell a snarky look. The two women exchanged giggles.

Dressed sharply in her signature white capris, Italian sandals, and a colorful flowing top, Eloise didn't miss a single beat as she carried her designer handbag elegantly draped on one arm.

"One must travel in style, Mitchell!" Eloise continued as she gave her perfectly coiffed hair a light bounce with her right hand.

"Yeah, yeah, I hear you, Your Highness," Mitchell shot back.

Elizabeth chuckled to herself watching her father and their longtime housekeeper get their kicks exchanging banter. After twenty-five years of living under the same roof, there were no-holds-barred between the two. Time had allowed them to become comfortable with their rants and bantering back and forth, often sounding more like two bickering or teasing siblings than adults.

The young woman stopped momentarily, adjusting her grip on her dog's pet carrier and her suitcase simultaneously. She let out a sigh and cleared her throat. As a freelance photographer, she was always diligent in making sure her camera and travel equipment were packed into a carry-on for security.

It never failed, however, carrying the weight of a dog in a pet carrier and camera equipment at the same time could certainly be daunting!

"You okay, honey?" asked her father, not missing a beat while watching his daughter struggling.

"Oh, yeah Dad, I'm fine," Elizabeth answered back, pacing herself, so she didn't feel too winded. "Just gathering my energy from our chaotic morning!"

Chaotic was an understatement!

Due to the storm, the trio sat stuck unexpectedly on the tarmac at the airport in North Carolina for hours. Mitchell, being the cautious planner he was, had tried to make sure they would have ample time to recover in Los Angeles. In the end, delays and adverse weather had defeated his meticulous travel planning.

Finally securing their boarding passes, they continued as quickly as they could to the security gates. Realizing it would take her longer to get through security with Tito, her beloved Yorkie in tow, Elizabeth encouraged Eloise and her father to continue to the boarding gate.

"Mitchell, you go ahead, let them know there are two more coming, I will stay here and wait for Liz."

"Are you sure, girls?" he called out as the two were still held up with the security officials.

"Yeah Dad, go ahead, we'll catch up!" Elizabeth hollered back as she motioned to her father to continue.

"Okay honey, will do." Mitchell turned to look at his boarding pass again to see which gate they were flying out.

"Oh gee, you have got to be kidding me!" he sighed.

As Murphy's Law would have it, their departure gate was located at the furthest end of the building.

Not wanting to miss a beat, the now-weary father adjusted his grip on his carry-on and hoisted his travel satchel back on his shoulder. Double checking to make sure his travel documents were still in hand, Mitchell pushed his glasses back up the bridge of his nose as he began a light jog down the airport hallway.

"Pardon, Miss," he exclaimed as he continued with a heavy breath, trying politely to pass fellow passengers, "on your left, sorry about that!" he apologized as he continued jogging toward the gate.

Mitchell couldn't help but mutter to himself, "Time to cut back on Elle's baked goods, Fisher!" The aging father took a quick look down to his slightly bouncing belly as he reached up to push his glasses back on his face.

Dressed in typical Hawaiian tourist attire, Mitchell patted down his brightly patterned shirt as he tried to focus on the crowds in front of him and not on his aging physique. His slip-on loafers gave a slight squeak on the highly-polished floor, and the rustling of his khakis made their signature 'swoosh-swoosh' as he continued.

After a good few minutes, Mitchell gave himself a break as he slowed his pace. As he stopped to make another adjustment to his traveling gear, he heard a loud beeping approaching from behind. Mitchell instinctively moved himself to hug the wall as the sound of an airport passenger cart came closer.

"We'd offer you a ride, Mitchell, but there's no more room!" Eloise waved her hand up as the cart whizzed by with the two women taking advantage of the buggy ride to the gate.

Elizabeth waved at her father as she sat in the back facing his direction with Tito and their luggage.

"We'll tell them to hold the plane for you, Mitchell!" Eloise hollered over her shoulder as the airport buggy maneuvered its way around other passengers.

"Yeah, thanks, ladies!" Mitchell hollered back sarcastically as he watched his daughter shrug her shoulders in guilt, knowing full well Eloise was up to her usual smart-ass antics!

4

~ * ~

"What in the heck is he doing?" Elizabeth gave Eloise a nudge as she watched her father get up and make his way to an empty aisle just in front of a row of passengers.

Eloise rolled her head slightly to the left as she watched Mitchell take a standing position with his back to the remaining seated passengers. Placing his hands firmly on his hips, the elder gentleman began slowly turning his upper body.

"Oh, Lord help us, he's gonna start doing his exercises!" Eloise rolled her eyes. Several times a day, at the advice of his doctor, Mitchell would take several moments to do various standing stretches.

Eloise continued to watch him, in obvious discomfort as she peered over her glasses.

"That is so embarrassing." Elizabeth couldn't help but laugh as she muttered in a muffled voice, watching her father lean forward and extend his arms in front of him, thrusting his backside out. "He's over there doing old man stretches in front of *everyone*...geez Dad...*stop!*"

"Don't do the squats, Mitchell, don't do the squats!" Eloise let out an exasperated sigh as they watched the row of three female passengers sitting directly behind him exchange glances with one another.

Elizabeth and Eloise strained to eavesdrop as they watched Mitchell turn to engage in conversation with the women.

"You'll have to excuse me," he said to the women seated directly behind him, "my doctor encourages me to do these stretches several times a day. Of course, in flight, it's very beneficial for the body to keep the blood flowing, especially at my age!"

His face slightly flushed with embarrassment, Mitchell turned his back to the group as he felt the intense burn of three pairs of eyes focused on him.

Elizabeth couldn't help but let out a snort as Eloise shook her head back and forth. They continued to watch as Mitchell bent forward to touch his toes, full derriere on display to the now-giggling group of women. Mitchell turned and gave them a sheepish grin as he made his way back to his seat. Glancing over at his daughter and her companion he shrugged his shoulders in the air.

"What?" he exclaimed, as he noted their expressions.

"Nothing!" Elizabeth tried to contain the smirk that had crept over her face, knowing full well the response that was readying itself from her travel companion.

"You, that's what!" Eloise stared at Mitchell as she slanted her eyes at him over the rim of her glasses. "Over there bending yourself forward in front of those poor girls. Having your big, old, you-know-what on full display, for heaven's sake!"

Mitchell brushed her comments off with a wave of his hand as she sat there shaking her head in obvious disagreement.

"You know my doctor recommends that I do those stretches for my blood flow, especially while traveling on a plane."

"Does your doctor also recommend you stick your butt out in people's faces?" Eloise retorted back, unable to resist the urge to egg him on.

Mitchell arranged his belongings in his seat, gathering his flight-issued pillow and blanket. He turned his back to Eloise as he adjusted his headset, giving her the cold shoulder. Not wanting to miss his opportunity he muttered just loud enough for her to hear him.

"Better it be my ass than yours!"

"I heard that Fisher!" Eloise shook her head as she went back to watching her movie, lowering her voice so as not to offend anyone seated near them. "Consider yourself lucky that's not where I'm sticking my foot, thank you very much!"

Mitchell chuckled to himself as he listened to Eloise rant. Making himself comfortable in his seat he plugged his headset back into the entertainment console. He continued to smile, as his humorous tiffs with her kept them both amused.

Elizabeth laughed as she watched the two people she loved the most in the world, egging each other on. Reaching down under the seat in front of her, she extended a few fingers into the portable pet carrier to give her Yorkshire Terrier a loving scratch under the chin. The calm and sleepy dog licked her fingers dutifully.

Sleepy herself, Elizabeth adjusted her travel sweater over her arms as she leaned her head onto Eloise's shoulder.

These were the lighthearted moments in her life that made Elizabeth truly grateful.

The young woman continued to relax on Eloise's shoulder as her eyes grew heavy. Slowly looking down at her companion's right arm, she noticed that Eloise was wearing her favorite bracelet. A beautiful yet modest gold bracelet adorned with tiny diamonds. A Christmas gift given to her by Elizabeth's mother just before her death.

Elizabeth would hold those memories in her heart and her mind forever. At the tender age of ten, that Christmas was the last one she would spend with her mother before she passed away from the complications of ovarian cancer.

Watching Elizabeth as she traced the interweaving gold metal of the bracelet with her forefinger, Eloise reached over and gently gave the young woman's hand a squeeze.

Eloise remembered those days after the loss of Mrs. Fisher like they were yesterday. She thought to herself, as she closed her eyes momentarily.

She had been asked to stay on in the household to help raise Elizabeth after her mother died, while the grieving widower buried himself in his dental practice. Eloise had known for many years that she was considered family.

Other than a paycheck left dutifully on the kitchen counter every Friday for twenty-five years, Eloise never felt like an employee of the Fishers. As a trained nursing assistant, she had been hired as a caregiver for Mitchell's terminally ill wife. She then followed through with the promise she made to Mrs. Fisher to stay on and help look after the widower and his young daughter.

Having been a widow herself after losing her beloved husband to a tragic accident, Eloise was empathetic to the pain the grieving family had gone through. With very little family herself, she felt blessed that the cards unfolded in her life the way they did. She was paid well to care for the homestead, more than she ever would have made working as just a nursing assistant.

The Fisher's hundred-year-old home in the coastal town of Wilmington, North Carolina had been intentionally remodeled to include separate living quarters just for Eloise at the request of the late Mrs. Fisher. She had developed a special bond with the young Georgian woman who had cared for her day and night until her death. Not that Eloise spent much time in it, other than to sleep. She spent most of her days and evenings in the main residence of the house. Having her meals with the Fishers to discuss the day's events, helping Elizabeth with her studies, or planning weekend outings to the local parks and beaches.

When Mitchell wasn't consumed with his practice, Eloise provided companionship to the widower, as they had developed a special bond after Joanna's death. Whether they were yelling at the television while watching a competitive sports game cheering for their favorite team or playing an intense game of chess, their competitive nature kept them both amused.

Mitchell was no stranger to reminding Eloise on a regular basis how much she meant to the family and how they could never imagine their lives without her.

For all her idiosyncrasies and sassy back-talk, she was, after all, the foundation that kept them all going.

There was a bond between the three of them that no one could ever break.

~ * ~

CHAPTER TWO ~ The Apple Incident

"Baby girl, wake up, we're almost there. Just look at the beauty that awaits us!" Eloise gently nudged Elizabeth out of her slumber.

Rubbing her eyes, she turned her head to gaze out of the airplane window.

What a sight to behold! Rugged yet majestic cliffs penetrated the vast, open skyline of the Hawaiian island. Lush green valleys could be seen cutting narrow passageways through the island's cliffs. The crystal blue, sparkling ocean waters gracefully lapped the imposing shoreline.

One couldn't help but tingle with excitement at the privilege of viewing such grandeur!

Elizabeth grinned as she looked over at her father. Sound asleep and snoring, she waited a few minutes to wake him. He would, after all, have plenty of time to take in the sights once they reached their destination of Kapalei, a quaint coastal town bordering the majestic cliffs of Na Pali.

"Dad, wake up, we're here!" Mitchell felt the gentle nudge on his shoulder from his daughter. He lifted his headset as he quickly glanced around the cabin of the airplane. Blinking several times, he realized they had, in fact, finally landed in Kauai.

Mitchell got his bearings as he watched Eloise and Elizabeth begin to gather their belongings from their seats and the overhead compartment. Other passengers were already well in pursuit of the exit door, carry-on luggage and children in tow.

Realizing that he must have fallen back to sleep immediately after his meal, Mitchell stood up to stretch his weary body. Glancing at his watch, he saw that it was only mid-afternoon. He knew his body needed a chance to adapt to the time zone difference as it was creeping up on his bedtime hour back on the East Coast.

"Don't you even think about bending over and touching your toes while the rest of us are trying to navigate around your old backside!" Eloise quipped as she cocked her head over her left shoulder, watching Mitchell intently as he stretched his arms out in front of him.

"Yeah, yeah, I hear ya!" He pursed his lips together after giving her a quick response. "I am just as ready as you ladies are to get off this plane!"

Mitchell looked on as his daughter juggled her carry-on bag and Tito's pet carrier.

"Honey, do you need help with anything?"

"No Dad, I'm okay, thanks. Oh, and before you ask, I feel fine!" Elizabeth gave him a quick wink.

Having been so worn out from the whirlwind of planning and preparing to leave the East Coast coupled with the craziness of the early part of their day, Elizabeth, like her father, had quickly fallen asleep on the last leg of their journey.

Mitchell smiled lovingly at his daughter as she began to make her way down the aisle, following Eloise's lead. Her pixie-short brown hair was neatly tucked behind her signature headscarf, with little wisps of bangs gently falling on her forehead. Her bright blue eyes now looking fresh and alert.

"Hey guys, I'm going to have to head down to Customs with Tito, can I meet you both in baggage claim?" Elizabeth asked Eloise and Mitchell as she stopped a few feet ahead of them.

"Hold on a minute," Mitchell called out as he pointed to a young woman near the gate holding a sign with the Fisher name written on it. "Don't forget to get your flowers, honey!"

Elizabeth smiled brightly as she headed in the direction of the young lady holding floral necklaces.

"Well, Mitchell, I am impressed!" Eloise smirked as she too, headed in the direction of the flower girl. "You thought of everything, didn't you?"

"Well, I wasn't going to start our trip without a customary lei!"

"I do hope you remembered that I prefer a subtle shade of wine with a hint of boysenberry."

"Yes, I know." Mitchell rolled his eyes at Eloise as she pointed to the designer bag strapped to her arm, adorned in her favorite color. "I am sure you will be very pleased with my selection as it compliments both your fashionable attire *and* your overly priced matching handbag!"

Eloise and Elizabeth both smiled as they modeled the beautiful floral necklaces Mitchell has chosen for them.

"I have trained you well, Mitchell Fisher!" Eloise quipped as she admired the pretty orchid lei around her neck.

13

"They're really nice Dad, thanks!" Elizabeth reached over to give her father a kiss on the cheek.

"Well, as they say, when in Rome, you do as the..." Mitchell started, only to be cut off mid-sentence.

"You have people waiting with designer Italian shoes for us then?" Eloise interrupted Mitchell as she snickered at her own joke.

Elizabeth laughed as she nodded her head in agreement. Designer shoes were one of Eloise's weakness in life, having more pairs in her closet then actual room for them. A bad habit Elizabeth admittedly started years prior when she would bring a box home for Eloise at Christmas or her birthday from her photo shoots in Italy.

"If you acquire another pair of Italian shoes I will be forced to add another addition onto the house just to fit them all!" Mitchell shot back as he laughed at her humor.

"A woman, Mitchell, can never have too many shoes." Eloise winked at Elizabeth as she continued her joke at Mitchell's expense.

The trio headed down the open and airy hallway towards the baggage claim area. Glancing at the various shops and décor, they got the feeling they were officially on a vacation island!

Elizabeth headed in the direction of the check-in with her canine companion, his veterinary paperwork in hand. Aware of the customs regulations, she wanted to ensure everything was in order so a quarantine would not be necessary.

"Mitchell, I am going to step to the ladies' room, I will meet you at the baggage carousel," Eloise called out over her shoulder, not waiting for a reply as she headed to the restroom.

Mitchell stood briefly as he watched the two ladies head in separate directions. Nodding his head at the disappearing backsides of both his daughter and his resident antagonist, Mitchell dutifully headed towards the baggage claim. Walking in unison with the dozens of other passengers from the flight, he quickly adjusted his pace with his carry-on roller and shoulder satchel.

Does this thing feel heavier or what? He thought to himself as he glanced down at the bag slung across his chest. Mitchell made another adjustment as he felt the contents of his bag shift from one side to the other, seemingly unaware of two, slightly bulging items pressing on the leather's exterior.

Mitchell took his position by the carousel as suitcases slowly started to trickle onto the moving conveyor belt. Numerous individuals took turns as they stooped over to retrieve their baggage.

Being the methodical person that he was, Mitchell always attached bright red travel tags to the family's checked luggage, ensuring they would have an easier time spotting their belongings. With so many similar bags, one could stand there forever overlooking their own suitcase by accident!

The first of several dark bags adorned with brightly colored tags were slowly inching their way in Mitchell's direction. Out of the corner of his eye, he took notice of two uniformed

15

airport security agents flanked by two large beagles making their way through the crowds.

Distracted with his current responsibility of retrieving their bags, he didn't give them much notice again until he felt a nudge on his leg. Looking down, he found himself staring eye-to-eye with one of the dogs. The beagle again nudged on his right leg as he quickly tried to shift his body weight, annoyed that the dog seemed intent on getting his attention. Then, without any warning, the dog began to bark incessantly.

"Sir, please remove your shoulder bag," commanded the stern voice of one of the security agents.

Now realizing the commotion was garnering an audience, Mitchell continued to clutch his satchel.

"What's going on, Officer, I don't understand?"

"Sir, we require that you remove your shoulder bag and place it on the floor, please." The other security personnel instructed.

"Can you please explain to me why I'm being interrogated and required to let you inspect my bag?"

"Sir, please do as we say, we don't want to have to ask you again." This time both agents had moved in closer to Mitchell, as though prepared to physically remove the bag.

"Don't you just think this is a bit ridiculous, I mean really, and will you please get your dog to stop jumping on my leg!"

Suddenly and without warning one of the two agents grabbed the bag, and attempted to forcefully remove it from Mitchell's grip. Out of pure instinct, Mitchell gripped the bag tightly and outstretched his arm to push the security agent away.

"Agent Kahele, request for backup in baggage claim, carousel six," called the other agent on a microphone attached to her shoulder.

Now realizing he had created a real scene with both dogs barking and numerous passengers staring in shock and bewilderment, Mitchell released his grip and began to remove the bag.

"Fine, fine, I will take the bag off!" Mitchell dropped the bag to the ground, not before seeing the figure of a very large and muscular man heading in his direction. Placing his hand on what appeared to be a gun, the agent was accompanied by what Mitchell swore was the largest German Shepherd dog he had ever seen in his life.

Like something out of a television drama, Mitchell stepped away from his bag, raising both hands in front of him.

"Okay guys, I don't want any trouble, but I honestly don't understand what this is all about!"

Agent Kahele approached Mitchell with a stern look on his face. Not waiting for permission, the ominous-looking agent let loose his dog as it scrambled for the bag. Seeing its snout disappear into the bag, it removed the contents, which appeared to be two, large apples.

Turning to look the confused passenger square in the eye, the intimidating agent retrieved the dog's leash as he picked up both apples with one hand.

"Sir, it is against the law to bring seeded, foreign fruit into the Territory of Hawaii. You will have to come with me."

"I don't understand, I mean, they came from an airport in the USA, we're still in the USA, I don't get what the problem is and honestly officer, I didn't even remember they were in there!"

"It's Agent, Sir...Agent Kahele and if you take a good look you will see they are clearly marked 'Fiji' on the label." The agent sternly replied as he held the label side up, narrowing his eyes at Mitchell. "Therefore, they are in fact, foreign seeded fruit."

Mitchell, still in shock, stood dumbfounded as he watched the other two agents gather his satchel and carry-on bag. At that very moment, Eloise had joined the large crowd that had gathered to watch incident that was unfolding.

"Mitchell, what in the heck is going on?"

Mitchell held both his hands in the air as he tried to keep her calm.

"Now, now Elle, don't worry, this is just all a big misunderstanding!"

"Ma'am, are the two of you traveling together?" Agent Kahele directed his question to the embarrassed-looking Eloise.

"Lord help me, yes, I'm traveling with that foolish man!"

"You will have to gather your belongings as well and come with us."

"All this spectacle over a damn piece of fruit!" Eloise couldn't help but curse as she gave Mitchell a death stare. The frustrated housekeeper gathered their bags and with the

18

assistance of one of the other agents, placed them on the rolling cart Mitchell had secured at the carousel. Letting out a huge and completely purposeful sigh, Eloise followed the group down the hall, pushing the cart.

Just at that moment, Elizabeth rushed to join them, out of breath from her jog down the hall.

"What's going on Dad?" She asked as she juggled her carry-on suitcase and Tito's carrier.

"Nothing honey, honestly. It's all just a huge misunderstanding, there's nothing to worry about."

The group entered a large room where the contents of all the bags were placed on a table as the two original security agents began the painstaking process of checking through every item.

"Honestly, Agent Kahele, I completely forgot I put those two pieces of fruit in my bag. I had no idea I couldn't bring fresh fruit into the airport!"

Before Agent Kahele had a chance to respond, Eloise turned to stare at Mitchell, both her hands still placed firmly on her hips as she was watching the security agents go through her things.

"What on Earth were you thinking? Did you not hear them say over the plane intercom telling everyone to dispose of all fresh fruit?"

"I had my headsets on Eloise, and I didn't hear that part."

"We flew into an airport on an isolated, remote island in the Pacific Ocean, Mitchell Fisher, common sense would tell you that they *might* have food restrictions!"

"Well, I didn't think I would be interrogated and have to declare a darn piece of fruit!" Mitchell retorted back.

"Um, yeah Dad, they have all that information in the fine print of the airline tickets also." Elizabeth also interjected into the conversation.

"Honey, I had my headset on, I didn't hear the announcement, and nobody ever reads the fine print. I honestly completely forgot they were in my bag."

"You didn't forget to stand up every hour on the hour to do your butt stretches in front of two hundred people. You'd think you would have remembered bagging two big ole pieces of fruit in your man purse!" Eloise continued to antagonize Mitchell.

"Enough people, that's enough!" Agent Kahele quickly motioned himself between Eloise and Mitchell, like a referee at a boxing match. "Clearly from the sounds of it, you obviously forgot you had them in your bag."

Standing a good six and a half feet tall, the agent towered over the bickering couple. Crossing his arms over his chest, he turned his attention back to Mitchell. Elizabeth, still seated nearest the door, continued to look on as though she was watching an afternoon soap opera.

"I'm a retired dentist, what can I say, I like to keep healthy fruit in my daily diet. Haven't any of you heard that old saying, 'An apple a day keeps the doctor away?' I mean, come on now," Mitchell attempted to crack a joke, "apples are good for you!"

20

"Sir, that's not funny, this is a serious matter. There are repercussions that can have a detrimental impact on our native ecology should foreign seeded fruit contaminate our environment." The man looked sternly at Mitchell.

Mitchell, now feeling ashamed, looked glumly at the pile of their belongings strew across the large table. "Well, I truly apologize Agent Kahele, I did not mean to cause all this commotion and confusion."

Feeling sorry for the older fellow, having witnessed his travel companions grill him, Agent Kahele lowered his arms to his hips and spoke in a softer tone.

"I will waive the fine I would normally write out for an incident like this. Just be careful next time, Mr. Fisher, and pay attention to the flight attendant's messages. You are all free to go."

The girls hurriedly gathered their bags. Wasting no time following their lead, Mitchell quickly gathered his things as they all scrambled for the door.

Once the trio had cleared the earshot of the security agents, Eloise took the opportunity to lay into Mitchell.

"I have never been so damn embarrassed in my whole life, Mitchell Carmichael Fisher, what the heck is wrong with you?"

"Uh, yeah Dad, that was pretty bad. I think everyone near baggage claims was filming this one! I'm pretty sure there will be some social media videos trending today."

"Oh, don't even get me started on that, Lord help us." Eloise shook her head back and forth as she contemplated the very notion of it. "If I wanted to be admired by millions, I would have become a dang movie star...now I'm going be infamously known as *that woman* with the Hawaiian Apple Fool!"

"Yep, it will probably get a few million hits by the weekend." Elizabeth couldn't help but make a wisecrack at the thought of it. "You even had to push that awkward cart with all your baggage, geez, talk about embarrassing, I wonder what the neighbors would think?"

"Missy, you are not helping matters any!" Eloise snapped at Elizabeth as she continued giving Mitchell the third degree.

"Honestly girls, let it go! I made a genuine mistake, and I'm sorry if it caused either of you any embarrassment. If anyone is going to look stupid on a viral social video making its rounds, it's going to be me!" Mitchell sighed heavily. All he wanted to do now was focus on getting the rental car and getting as far away from the scene of the unfortunate incident as quickly as he could!

"*Um hum*," Eloise muttered under her breath as she walked ahead of Mitchell and Elizabeth down the corridor, her orchid lei bouncing on her chest as she upped her pace. "I'm not talking to you right now, Mitchell Fisher!"

"You, quiet for five minutes, voluntarily...really?" Mitchell took the shot that was presented to him. "How did I ever get so lucky?"

Eloise gave Mitchell an ugly look as she abruptly turned her head to the side, refusing to make eye contact with him.

"Okay, kids, time to play nicely!" Elizabeth interjected as she broke up the squabbling pair, something she was all too familiar with doing.

She stopped dead in her tracks as she pointed her forefinger to the large sliding glass doors. "Come on guys, stop with the bickering and look out the window at where we are!"

Just beyond the steel-beamed ceiling and the waiting benches was a warm and inviting late afternoon. A mild breeze could be felt making its way into the open corridor, carrying with it a light fragrance from the numerous flowers planted around the exterior of the airport.

Several minutes later, after a check-in at the car rental counter, the group headed to the parking lot.

"Well, here we are." Mitchell stopped next to a bright red, shiny new convertible car. "As I have said before when in Rome do as the Romans do. So, I figured, if we're going to be staying on an island, why not a convertible!"

The two women stood by the vehicle, clearly impressed with Mitchell's selection.

"Dad, I honestly had you pegged as sporting us around in something...well, how do I put this nicely, cheap!"

"I know you did honey," Mitchell answered his daughter in a very matter of fact manner, "I just figured, I mean, since we are going to be here for a while, why not something fun?"

"Well, well Fisher, trying to get back in my good graces, are you?" Eloise cocked her head down slightly as she lowered her sunglasses while looking at Mitchell, one eyebrow slightly raised.

"Did it work?"

"I don't know, are you gonna give me the keys so I can drive?"

"Um, no...but it would be nice if you would forgive me for my shortcomings anyway."

"Let me cruise for a while with the top down, the fresh air can clear the pains in my head you caused me today, and I'll think about it." Eloise quipped as she and Elizabeth let Mitchell load their suitcases into the trunk.

"Dad, will everything fit?" Elizabeth asked inquisitively as her father struggled to pack all their checked luggage into the tiny trunk.

"Don't even get me started on *why* it might not fit!" Mitchell pursed his lips together as he looked directly as Eloise.

Purposely ignoring his comment, Eloise gracefully sank into the bucket seat of the sporty car.

"Here, Dad, just put the rest in the backseat with me. I'll put Tito on my lap." Elizabeth offered as she smiled at her thoroughly exhausted father.

Mitchell gave his daughter a gentle pat on the back as she climbed into the back seat. Adjusting his sunglasses on the bridge of his nose, he started the ignition. Checking all the mirrors and setting the navigation system, he searched for the button to release the convertible top.

Eloise clapped her hands together, "Now we're talking!"

Putting the car into gear, Mitchell slowly navigated the vehicle through the airport exit and onto the highway.

"Do you wanna get there in one hour or five, Mitchell?"

"I just want to be extra cautious, this is, after all, a brand-new vehicle."

"You have a V-8 engine under the hood, so drive this thing like it was designed to be driven…do not make me feel like one of those old people on the road that pokes along at a snail's pace!"

The trio allowed themselves the enjoyment of absorbing the late afternoon sun and the scenic drive up the highway to their destination. The winding road often juggled between densely, vegetated areas that would give way to open flatland. All the while enjoying a periodic glimpse at the ocean, a flowing river and of course, the amazing island cliffs as they passed by the never-ending terrain of forest reserves.

A good thirty minutes into their drive, Mitchell gave an update on their location and the proximity to their rental house.

"Not long now girls!" He bellowed happily from the driver's seat as he attempted to talk over the wind tunneling its way through the open-topped vehicle.

"What was that?" Elizabeth called out from the backseat, trying to lean forward to hear what her father had just said.

Turning to look over his shoulder, Mitchell repeated himself a bit louder.

Just at that moment, Elizabeth's attention was focused on a fast-moving vehicle, failing to yield at an oncoming intersection. Her eyes grew wide as she gasped, realizing what was about to happen.

"Oh, my God, look out!" Elizabeth hollered from the back seat as she watched the unavoidable situation that was about to unfold.

~ * ~

CHAPTER THREE ~ You Don't Mess with Kahele

Everyone instinctively screamed as a large, white vehicle, having failed to yield at its stop sign, proceeded to pull out in front of the newly rented convertible.

The car brakes screeched as the flashy red car spun in a circle in the busy intersection.

"Sweet Jesus, don't hit the truck!" Eloise screamed as she clutched the car door with one hand and the console with the other.

Mitchell attempted with all his might to maneuver the vehicle away from the oncoming truck. Narrowly missing getting side slammed, the convertible finally came to a stop on a grassy patch adjacent to the road. Almost simultaneously a loud 'BOOM' could be heard as the white vehicle made an impact with the back of a fruit truck.

Within seconds a rain of what appeared to be guavas came showering down on the trio from out of the sky. A dozen or so of the round, green fruit randomly struck areas within the car, while a few stragglers landed on the hood of their vehicle.

Throwing their arms up to avoid being pummeled by flying fruit, the three passengers sat stunned in their seats.

Completely in shock at the sudden event that could have claimed the lives of the vehicle occupants, Mitchell quickly regained his senses.

"Eloise, Elizabeth honey, are you both okay?" Mitchell turned abruptly to check on his daughter sitting in the back seat clutching her dog to her chest, her eyes wide as her body and mind were still comprehending what had just happened.

"Yeah, Dad, we're okay," His daughter answered softly, still dazed by the near-miss on the road.

"Eloise, are you alright?" Mitchell leaned forward to check on his companion sitting motionless in the passenger seat, clutching the doorframe and console.

Eloise glanced up at Mitchell, just before turning her head as far as she could to catch a glimpse of the vehicle that had clipped the back end of the fruit truck.

"I suppose you were wrong, Elle, not all old people poke along at a snail's pace!"

"What *the hell* was that woman thinking?" Eloise fired up as the shock of the situation got the better of her emotions. "Pulling out in front of people like that? I mean, she didn't even bother to stop! She just *rolled* on through like she was the queen of the freaking highway! Don't even get me started on the fact that we all just nearly got knocked the heck out by flying fruit!"

Angrily, Eloise collected a couple of guavas as she looked prepared to exit the vehicle, combat fruit in hand.

Mitchell rubbed his unshaven face as he surveyed the scene. Apparently uninjured, the elderly woman had gotten out of her car and appeared to be arguing with the driver of the truck. Another vehicle slowly approached the scene, pulling over to assist.

"Stay here guys, let me go over and see if everyone is alright. Elizabeth, honey, call 911 and let them know there's been a car accident, and everyone appears to be okay, but assistance is needed."

Nodding her head, she hurriedly rummaged through her purse for a phone and proceeded to dial emergency services.

"Elle, stay in the car…I think it would be best if you don't create a scene. I will handle this." Mitchell put his hand firmly on Eloise's left arm.

"Oh, I'm not getting out of this car, I know I will say or do something I might regret to that blind, lead-foot-driving old bat!" Eloise continued to mutter as Elizabeth gave the emergency operator the information needed to find their location.

Mitchell stretched for a moment as he exited the convertible, to make sure everything was in working order. He then proceeded to cross the road to check on the occupants of the other vehicles. As he approached, he distinctively saw the woman pointing in his direction. Waving her arms, it appeared as though she was placing blame on him.

"Is everyone okay here, anybody hurt?" Mitchell asked solemnly.

"You were speeding!" The elderly lady wasted no time making accusations at Mitchell. Clutching her purse in one hand, she pointed to the significantly damaged white vehicle she had been driving.

"Now, now wait a minute ma'am." Mitchell put his hands up as he responded to her accusations. "I know, for a fact, I wasn't speeding. You failed to yield at your stop sign and pulled out in front of me."

"No, I most certainly did not!" The woman appeared as though she had just come from a round of golf somewhere, as she was wearing what looked like golf attire coupled with a visor cap and golf driver gloves.

Mitchell moved slightly closer to the woman, who was still rambling on about the accident being his fault.

Was that alcohol he could smell on her breath?

Attempting to get a little closer to confirm his suspicions, the woman suddenly and without warning began to swing at Mitchell with her purse.

"Don't you get near me you hooligan!" she hollered, striking Mitchell in the shoulder and chest with her purse.

"Lady, what in the hell is wrong with you?" Mitchell instinctively reached out to grab her purse as she continued to take swings at him. The driver of the truck, taken off guard by the old woman's sudden behavior, also tried to reach out and catch her purse as it made passes in the air.

"Lady, stop hitting me with your damn purse!" Mitchell was finally able to secure a hold on the purse as he jerked it away from her. Just at that very moment, sirens could be heard advancing towards the intersection. Police officers exited their vehicle and began to make their way towards the chaotic scene. As Mitchell turned to keep the woman from grabbing her bag, the button popped open as the contents fell onto the street.

"Now look what you did, officers, arrest this man! He caused me to wreck my car and assaulted me!" She hollered in her best 'woe-is-me' voice. The officers by this time had approached the group and gave Mitchell a suspicious look.

"I didn't do anything, I swear!" Mitchell dropped the bag onto the street as he put his hands up in front of him in self-defense. "It was her fault honestly, she pulled out in front of me and didn't even bother to stop, and I'm pretty sure she's been drinking!"

"I most certainly have not, you liar!" the woman retorted back, showing obvious signs that Mitchell had been correct as she slurred her words.

The silent fruit truck driver, spoke up for the first time, as he nodded in agreement with Mitchell, "Yeah man, pretty sure she's been tippin' the bottle somewhere bro, and she definitely pulled out in front of this dude."

The young driver continued to nod his head, all the while taking a few steps back from the old lady, as he was unsure of whether he would be on the receiving end of her flailing hands.

"We will need everyone to come down the station to file a report." One of the officers announced to the group. "Ma'am, you will have to ride with us."

They led her towards their vehicle, listening to her clearly object, but aware of the smell of alcohol on her. Mitchell and the truck driver nodded in agreement. By then, the ambulance had arrived, and the two were asked by medics if they needed any treatment. Across the road, another medic was checking on Eloise and Elizabeth.

"I'm okay guys, thanks. I don't think there is anything you can do for my nerves right now!" Mitchell attempted in vain to make a wisecrack.

Wow, what a horrendous day!

Mitchell made his way back to the convertible as he informed the girls he would have to make a statement at the police station.

"The audacity of that woman!" Mitchell, still in shock, shook his head in disbelief. First, to blatantly lie and try to accuse him of causing the accident, but then to have the nerve to hit him with her purse!

Following the police car a few miles down the road to the station, Mitchell parked the car under a shady tree.

"Girls, I'm sure this won't take long, why don't you both just rest okay?"

Elizabeth and Eloise nodded their heads, too exhausted to be bothered going into the police station or arguing with Mitchell about it. They both made themselves comfortable and shut their eyes, attempting to take a small, recovery nap.

Mitchell proceeded across the parking lot as a light breeze massaged his face. He closed his eyes momentarily to enjoy the feeling of the warm air.

Entering the police station, Mitchell took a seat at the direction of an officer behind the counter. Mitchell was informed that he would have to wait a few moments as the officer in charge was questioning the elderly woman involved in the accident.

After what seemed like an eternity, Mitchell looked up from the magazine he had begun to read and realized who the officer in charge was.

"You have got to be kidding me," he muttered to himself, rolling his eyes.

"Well, Mr. Fisher, we meet again, do we?"

Mitchell couldn't believe his dumb luck. It was Agent Kahele, the interrogating customs agent from the airport!

"Come with me, into my office. I have some questions I need to ask you." Agent Kahele motioned his hand towards the office door.

Mitchell reluctantly gathered his energy as he slowly made his way down the brightly lit hallway.

"Mr. Fisher, seems you have had a busy day today." The muscle-bound, uniformed civil servant let out a sarcastic grunt as he addressed Mitchell, who had slumped sheepishly down in his chair.

"Agent Kahele," Mitchell began as he attempted to explain his side of the story, "it's not how it looks!"

"Officer Kahele." The customs agent turned police officer lifted his wrist, taking a good look at his watch, then concentrated his stare back on Mitchell. "As of six o'clock this afternoon, it's Officer Kahele. I work two jobs to protect the vested interests of our fine island.

"Oh, okay, I got it." Mitchell tried to interject some humor into the already awkward situation, "See, I thought there were two of you...two really, big guys in uniform running around. Like, a twin or something."

"Do you see me laughing Mr. Fisher?"

"Sorry, yeah, that wasn't very appropriate."

"You do realize this is a not-so-funny situation, Mr. Fisher. First, you attempt to smuggle exotic fruit into our humble

33

island, and now you're accused of attacking an elderly female citizen." Officer Kahele stared intently at the older gentleman.

"Um, yeah, it doesn't sound great when you put it in that context." Mitchell clasped his hands together tightly in his lap.

"In all fairness, she did attack me first," Mitchell attempted to defend himself. "I mean, I have witnesses who saw her attack me first with her purse after she illegally cut me off in traffic!"

"Yes, I am aware of that, which is why I will let you off the hook…this time." Office Kahele narrowed his eyes at Mitchell. "Do remember, however, I will be watching you."

Mitchell's eyes grew wide as he watched the Officer give him the 'I'm watching you' motion with his hands.

"You're free to go, Mr. Fisher, let's not let this happen again."

Officer Kahele stood up from his seat behind his desk and opened the door for Mitchell to leave.

Jumping out of his chair, he made a beeline for the door. Not wanting to spend another moment in Officer Kahele's presence, he hustled his way out of the office.

Mitchell walked as quickly as he could down the sparsely populated police station hallway. Adjusting his sunglasses against the bright island sunshine, he briskly made his way to the convertible parked in the shade of a large Pacific Rosewood. Sitting in the driver seat, Elizabeth pointed her forefinger to the back where Tito had made himself comfortable curled into a little ball.

"Guess I have been relegated to the back seat, eh?" Mitchell asked sheepishly as he reached out for the door handle.

"You have guessed correctly," Eloise muttered in her no-nonsense voice, pursing her lips together as she crossed her arms over her chest.

"Ah, yeah Dad, you can pretty much say you lost your driving privileges for the day!" Elizabeth answered firmly, as she started the ignition, waiting for her father to settle into the back seat.

Mitchell fastened his seatbelt as he looked down at Tito.

"Well, at least you're not mad at me."

Responding in a sharp, yappy bark, Mitchell put both hands up in the air, as he was obviously wrong.

The trio rode in silence as the convertible made its way down the winding, sun-drenched road.

Just as well they sit in silence, they all thought to themselves. It had been a hectic twenty-four hours, and they needed some mental rest!

The car slowly approached a well-manicured, tree-lined road, as the navigation system announced their arrival to their destination. The group admired the beautifully landscaped lawns of several homes before reaching the end of the street, where Elizabeth maneuvered the vehicle into a driveway.

The trio smiled as they admired the stunning home Elizabeth had rented for them.

"Well, you sure do have fine taste, my dear!" Eloise clapped her hands together as she exited the vehicle, excitedly absorbing her surroundings.

One could not help but be in awe of the gorgeous property. Lush plants and flowers surrounded the house and grounds, giving way to a large pool and lounging patio area. The extended garden area was accented with strategically-placed seating arrangements so admirers could relax and take in the panoramic views overlooking the ocean.

"Will you guys please forgive me for the craziness I caused today?" The weary father tried in vain to get everyone to forgive him for his foolish actions.

"Only because I am happy to put my feet up and relax, do I forgive you, Fisher!" Eloise lowered her head as she stared Mitchell directly in the eyes from her standing position next to his still-seated one.

"It's gonna cost you, Dad!" His daughter piped up as she popped the trunk of the car.

"How about dinner somewhere nice tonight girls," Michell continued his plea for forgiveness, "your pick!"

"Alright, we forgive you!" Elizabeth leaned over the backseat to put her arms around her father's neck and gave him a big bear hug, knowing full well the elder Fisher felt terrible for their day's events.

"I just want my seafood and a margarita!" Eloise stood in the driveway with her hand on her hip, pointing her finger at Mitchell.

"Done!"

Tito barked enthusiastically as he stretched his body, eager to get in on the action.

"Oh, and I promise we will bring you home something delicious to eat Mr. Tito Tito Bo Bito. I am so ready to put these last twenty-four hours behind us!"

~ * ~

CHAPTER FOUR ~ The Comforts of Home

Gathering their luggage, the group made their way up the stone-laid steps to the foyer of the beautiful home. Using the keycode entry given to her by the property management company, Elizabeth unlocked the large, glass-accented mahogany door. The family smiled in unison as they admired their surroundings, which would be their home for the next month.

Gorgeous hardwood floors reflected a splendid sheen from the overhead lighting. Comfortable, high-end furniture adorned the house, the walls of which were comprised of mainly glass panels.

"Well, there certainly is no shortage of breathtaking views of the ocean from anywhere in this home!" Eloise exclaimed as she took in the stunning garden accented by palm trees whose leaves lightly swayed in the late afternoon breeze.

"Oh, my heavens and just *look* at that kitchen!" She excitedly raced over to the room where she would be spending much of her time. She admired the stainless-steel kitchenware and highly polished stone countertop accented by beautiful, dark mahogany cabinets.

"Oh look, there's even a hammock!" Mitchell set his belongings down as he unlocked a patio door to exit out to the back of the home. Eloise and Elizabeth watched Mitchell wander out from the spacious sitting room. A long, curved sofa and a variety of artwork complimented the expansive room done in subtle hues of cream, beige and brown.

"Well, well, my sweet girl, you sure outdid yourself this time!" Eloise draped an arm over her shoulder, complimenting Elizabeth on her choice

The young woman watched intently as her father made his way back to the massive living room.

"You did an excellent job finding this one honey."

"Oh, thanks, Dad, you and Elle deserve it." Elizabeth approached her father and gave him an extended hug. "Happy retirement!"

Mitchell gave his daughter a peck on the cheek as Eloise made her way back into the kitchen.

"Child, you obviously thought of everything, there's even food in the fridge!" Eloise was beaming, grateful she wouldn't have to be up at the crack of dawn making a run down to the local supermarket.

"Yeah, I called the property management company yesterday. They have a shopping service they offer, so folks don't have to worry about showing up to a rental with an empty kitchen. You just do the grocery shopping online, and they pick it up!"

"Well now, that is convenient!" Eloise replied impressed.

"Okay girls, you two go and pick your rooms out so we can get washed up and on our way to eat." Mitchell clasped his hands together as he watched the two women scramble down the hallway.

Not surprisingly, all the bedrooms in the house had north facing windows and sliding glass doors, each leading out to the garden patio overlooking the stunning coastline.

One could get certainly get used to this lifestyle!

A decision had been made on just a simple seafood dinner somewhere close to the house that evening, as the time was already creeping up on eight o'clock and they all agreed, they were exhausted!

Elizabeth made Tito comfortable in her bedroom, ensuring he had a dish of his food and water readily available as she headed out the door with Eloise and her father.

"Eloise, dear," Mitchell walked towards the driver's side of the car then paused briefly to dangle the keys in the air, "would you like to drive?"

"Mitchell, dearest, seeing that you haven't been completely banned from driving, you can continue with the chauffer service. I am far too beat to wanna concentrate on any driving!" She gave him a genuine smile as she slid into the passenger seat.

Having changed into a comfortable, dark blue chiffon two-piece set, Eloise adjusted the large, gold plated necklace that adorned her neckline as she reached forward to fix the straps on yet another pair of sandals.

Elizabeth decided to keep it casual with just a simple tee-shirt and cargo pants, replacing her headscarf with a tiny headband instead. Almost always make-up free, the young woman embraced the natural, 'I don't care about my appearance' mentality. Given her line of profession, often she would be out in remote locations, surrounded by the elements of just the Earth. Getting all dolled up in makeup and jewelry was something she simply didn't want to be bothered doing.

"Let's get this bad boy in motion Mitchell, I am *starving*!" Eloise piped up as she was still leaning forward in her seat adjusting her shoe straps.

Fifteen minutes later, having arrived at the restaurant, the group all but slumped down in their chairs. Agreeing not to discuss the day's events so they could enjoy a peaceful meal, they spent the time talking about how pretty the island was and how excited they all were to finally be there!

They were thoroughly enjoying the delicious food as they dined under a gorgeous, sunset sky. Sitting out on the open veranda, the trio gazed in awe at the landscape which created the backdrop of the restaurant.

Strategically located next to Kapalei Bay, the late evening breeze taunted and teased its way through the veranda as palm trees swayed amongst the forefront of the breathtaking coastline, giving way to the serenity of the gentle-sounding ocean as it lapped the shore. Late evening beachgoers could be seen dotting the sandy shore. In the distance, the awe-inspiring pinnacles of the Na Pali coast dominated the skyline.

Reaching for their cell phones, Eloise and Elizabeth wasted no time taking several photographs on their camera phones before the sun setting sky turned to darkness.

"And to think Dad, we may have ended up in boring old Florida instead!" Elizabeth grinned as she teased her father. Eloise and Elizabeth didn't have anything against Mitchell's choice for their holiday, the girls just decided that after many years spent taking family holidays to the popular Gulf Coast state, it was time for a change!

As a Christmas present, Elizabeth had gifted Eloise and her father a holiday retreat to their place of choice, after his official retirement from the dental practice he had founded thirty years prior. Wanting to take a sabbatical from work herself, Elizabeth had been saving for years to set enough money aside to cover travel costs, the rental property and spending money for the lengthy holiday stay.

The only thing that had fallen short of meticulous planning was the fact that Mitchell and Eloise would be up in each other's business now, every day, all day! Then again, no matter where they were, this was inevitable now that Mitchell was no longer spending his days and evenings at work.

Thankfully, Eloise spend a great deal of time at her parish church volunteering with other parishioners in various charitable activities.

Mitchell admired her dedication to her faith and to helping those in need. After giving it some thought, Mitchell began offering his services to fixed-income families and those less fortunate. He volunteered with a group of medical professionals who provided weekly services for free to those whom couldn't otherwise afford proper health care.

This was something that Mitchell was honored to do, and he knew, had his late wife been alive, she would have been especially proud. As an elementary school teacher, Joanna had been a kind and generous soul whose untimely death not only affected their family but the community, teachers, and students that knew her. Her passing had been felt by many.

"Good Lord, help us all if I had to spend another summer holiday watching college kids dressed as animated cartoon characters waddle around an overpriced resort saturated with exhausted parents and crying children!"

Elizabeth laughed as she watched her father give them a slight roll of the eyes. Mitchell had purchased a timeshare in Orlando, Florida when his daughter was young so the family could enjoy holidays at the entertainment parks as she was growing up. Mitchell would find time to take in a round of golf or take his daughter to the theme parks. Eloise, for her part, would opt to stay back at the timeshare dipping her feet in the pool and enjoying a delightful book.

"Well, thankfully, the two of you came to a decision before I had to pull the plug on the whole idea!" Elizabeth reprimanded her two companions. "Leave it to the flip of a quarter to resolve any squabble between children!"

Elizabeth smirked as she teased them both. When Mitchell and Eloise couldn't amicably decide on the something mutually, she would often resort to 'The Quarter' to solve any discrepancies between the two. As luck would have it, heads won and so did Eloise on her choice of Hawaii.

The drama, however, did not end there!

The next arduous task was getting the two of them to decide on *which island* the three of them would spend their holiday.

As usual, Elizabeth was forced to play mediator as her father chose Kauai and Eloise settled on Maui.

After another flip of the trusty quarter, Kauai was the winner, and Eloise accepted Kauai as the destination.

"I wasn't going to complain," Eloise recalled as they were finishing their meal with a tasty dessert, "I'm not sitting here being waved at by an overgrown mouse wearing double-buttoned, red britches, and that's all I care about!"

~ * ~

Later that evening after everyone had retired to their rooms, Elizabeth quietly made her way to her bathroom with a glass of water. Rummaging through her bag, she removed the medication bottles she had been looking for.

Standing in front of the mirror, she slowly moved her hand across her face as she slipped into a near trance of deep thought. She was so worn out from the whirlwind of planning and preparing to leave the East Coast, coupled with the craziness of their actual trip, Elizabeth was extremely surprised she wasn't completely wiped out.

More surprising, she had not gotten dizzy or nauseous from her medication on their flights. Her last few trips had not gone as well, sending her to the bathroom to regurgitate her food not long after attempting to eat.

Elizabeth sighed heavily as she removed the pills from their bottles and quickly chugged them down with the glass of water.

"Tomorrow is another day," she reassured herself with a positive mindset as she slowly climbed into the comfortable and inviting bed, "you're still here, and that's all that matters!"

~ * ~

CHAPTER FIVE ~ Mitchell Meets Walter

Elizabeth gave her father and Eloise a quick hug as she headed out the door, her yoga mat in hand. Never traveling without her trusty mat, she gave Tito a quick scratch behind the ears as he dutifully sat at the front door to see her off. Before their travels, Elizabeth had tracked down a reputable and highly recommended yoga instructor, a British woman who offered therapeutic yoga classes outdoors. Classes were held on the beach and on paddleboards, a new variation of the practice that Elizabeth recently found she thoroughly enjoyed!

Seemingly satisfied she was on her way, the little dog clicked his way across the hardwood floors to the travel carrier Elizabeth had set up in the living room for him to nap in during the day.

Enjoying a vantage point facing the opened sliding doors, the obedient Yorkie pawed at his blanket until he found himself a comfortable, curled up position. Occasionally he lifted his head to enjoy the many smells that made their way into the house, carried by the light, ocean breeze.

"Is it just me, or has that child been acting a bit reclusive since she arrived back home in Wilmington?" Eloise looked squarely at Mitchell as she dished her signature blueberry pancakes onto a plate, passing it across the kitchen counter to Mitchell. "She looks, I don't know, like she's been under the weather perhaps. She certainly needs some sun, I have never seen the child look so pasty!"

"I know what you mean, I noticed it too. I've been asking her if she's been feeling okay and she said 'yes', so I have to give her some space and not make her feel like I'm nagging," Mitchell answered as he reached for the cup of syrup, putting his newspaper down momentarily.

"You don't think there's something going on we don't know about, do you?"

"I'm sure if something were seriously wrong, she would tell us. I mean, I hope she would anyway."

"You don't think it's…" Eloise started her sentence only to have Mitchell quickly intercept her thought process.

"Let's not even engage the idea, Elle! She took all the preemptive measures the doctors told her to take, and she hasn't said anything to me since she had the surgeries. They gave her a clean bill of health on her last physical. I know my daughter, if something's going on, she would tell me."

"Okay, okay, I'm sure you're right," Eloise answered, not wanting to rock the boat with Mitchell on the sensitive subject.

Reaching for her coffee, she hoisted herself up onto a bar stool at the kitchen counter and promptly reached for the social section of Mitchell's newspaper.

"I thought when Elizabeth gets back we could all take a stroll down Main Street and have a look around," Mitchell spoke up as he peered over his reading glasses at Eloise, who was deeply engaged in the entertainment section of the newspaper. He listened momentarily as she mumbled to herself about the who's who of the celebrity world, a hobby she indulged in daily.

"Is there shopping involved in this stroll on Main Street?" she replied, not bothering to look up from her gossip column.

"Of course."

"Sounds good to me!"

"Promise me something," Mitchell pressed Eloise firmly on the matter, "Promise you won't badger Liz about anything when she gets back."

"Is there a pair of shiny new sandals involved in that request?"

"Are you asking me to bribe you?"

"I am merely saying that I am more inclined not to open my mouth if I am distracted by...oh, I don't know, a credit card and a boutique."

Mitchell reached for his wallet as he pulled out one of his credit cards. Mitchell kept his trusty 'bribe card' on hand for Eloise. It never failed, if he wanted her to stay quiet about something important, he would need leverage.

"Preferably under a hundred please," he made a point to say as he released his grip from the plastic object.

"Would you like me to stay quiet for one day or one week?"

Mitchell raised his eyebrow again, and he tilted his head to the side looking at her, as he thought for a moment.

"Fine, two hundred and you don't say anything...period!"

Eloise gave him a wide smile as she tucked the card into the front of her blouse. Mitchell rolled his eyes, as he shook his head, trying not to laugh. She was known for keeping more than credit cards in her safe spot. On the odd occasion, cash or even a cell phone had been found strategically placed within the easy reach of her undergarments.

"Pleasure doing business with you," she smirked as she headed towards the kitchen sink with her empty breakfast plate.

"Yeah, yeah, yeah," he muttered more to himself than her. "Are you sure we weren't married in another life or something? I mean, if I didn't know any better, I'd swear I was being duped like a husband to a wife who knows how to play the system in her favor!"

"Mitchell honey, don't flatter yourself, you *know* you are not my type!"

"Why would you say that?"

"If we were married, do you think I would honestly let you out of the house wearing those *ridiculous* shirts?" Eloise retorted as she pointed at his colorful attire.

Mitchell stood up defiantly as he puffed his chest out with his hands on his hips.

"There is nothing wrong with my clothes!" he answered as he continued walking around the breakfast room, pretending to strut his stuff like a proud peacock.

"Lord help me, Fisher, how I managed the last twenty-five years!" Eloise rolled her eyes as she returned to the kitchen.

Mitchell headed with his newspaper to the garden patio, Tito in tow. Sliding his sunglasses on his face, he turned back briefly to his companion, still hanging out in the kitchen. Pulling the credit card out of its strategic hiding place, she pretended to kiss it before returning it to its safe-keeping spot.

Leave it to Eloise to improvise to get what she wanted!

~ * ~

Not long after Elizabeth returned home from her first session of beach yoga, she hurried to change for their outing into town. Mitchell had the top down as the trio made their way out of their new neighborhood, enjoying the beautiful island weather.

"Be on the lookout for any large, white road tanks bearing the mark of an old lady in golf gear!" Eloise attempted a wisecrack at the events of their previous day.

"Let's hope she keeps her purse to herself!" Mitchell quipped back.

They slowly cruised their way into the small yet inviting town of Kapalei. Colorfully painted craft shops dotted the road as they passed by several businesses. Tourists and locals alike meandered their way up and down the busy street.

"Here, Dad, this looks like a good spot," Elizabeth called out from the backseat, having eyed a few shops she was keen to check out. Always one to admire the works of other fellow artists, a few galleries had caught her attention.

After finding a parking spot, the three of them wandered down the street together. Coming to a stop sign, Elizabeth immediately headed in one direction as Eloise turned to head in the opposite direction.

Mitchell stood there for a moment, aware he was now standing alone. He watched as his daughter waved out, hollering over her shoulder, "I'll find you guys!"

Observing Eloise as she sauntered her way towards a clothing boutique, he watched in amusement as she twirled around pulling the credit card out from her undergarment. Pointing to the shop, she jiggled her fingers in her trademark 'bye-bye' wave as she turned to head for the door.

Mitchell pursed his lips together as he realized he had just been dumped by both his daughter and his housekeeper in exchange for photography, paintings, and shoes!

Standing there for a moment with his hands on his hips, Mitchell surveyed the street and decided on his next move. Numerous eclectic shops displaying arts and crafts, clothing boutiques, and kayak rentals intermingled with coffee shops and an array of restaurants.

Noticing the straw-covered rooftop of what appeared to be a tiki bar, Mitchell shrugged his shoulders. He had, after all, been passed up for the companionship of fine art and boutique clothing, why not relax with a cold beer!

Mitchell adjusted his baseball cap over his neatly trimmed salt and pepper hair. Fitting his sunglasses into place, he patted down another one of Eloise's ill-favored foes, his colorful Hawaiian shirt, as he double-checked his back pocket for his wallet. Sporting a pair of jeans shorts, white calf length socks, and sneakers, and looking every inch the typical tourist, Mitchell meandered towards the bar.

"Who does she think she is, to say I have no style," he muttered to himself smugly as he sucked in his belly and slightly puffed out his chest, "there is nothing wrong with your style, Fisher!"

Mitchell winked at a young woman crossing the street, shopping bags in hand. She raised both eyebrows as she paused briefly, staring at Mitchell then quickly glancing over her shoulder at an attractive, well-muscled young man jogging to catch up to her. Mitchell nodded his head as he quickened his pace, embarrassed at his sudden attempts to appeal the opposite sex. Not wasting another second to even look over his shoulder, Mitchell quickly ducked his way into the relaxing environment of the bar, grateful Eloise hadn't just witnessed his little escapade!

Mitchell took notice of his surroundings as he slid himself into a seat at the bar.

A colorful, well-lit room with high pitched ceilings decorated with Polynesian-style décor, the business offered a homey feel almost immediately. One wall was fully opened to the elements of the weather, and a warm breeze could be felt passing through as Mitchell removed his cap and placed it on the counter next to him. Dining tables with patrons enjoying a sandwich or drink were clustered together within the small, central room. An elevated stage stood out in the corner, with a microphone and a few speakers pushed tightly against the back wall.

"Ah, and that would be the resident karaoke stage!" Mitchell grinned as he found himself mumbling aloud. Get Eloise down here and tipsy from a few alcoholic beverages, and she would spend hours up there entertaining the masses! An accomplished singer in her own right, Mitchell always did enjoy coming home from work to hear Eloise singing her favorite songs to the radio as she made the family their evening meals.

Mitchell continued to look around, taking notice of several colorful, orb-shaped lanterns hung from the wooden-beamed, pitched-roof ceiling while an eclectic display of artwork littered various wall space. A vintage surfboard that doubled as a sign was propped over the bar. Matching another surfboard sign outside, it read, 'Walter's by the Water' in a brightly-colored paint.

"What can I do you for, young man?" Mitchell heard a husky voice from behind.

Turning himself back around, Mitchell took notice of the friendly face in front of him.

A gentleman about the same age as himself was leaning over the custom-carved, wooden bar. Tanned from years of island weather with tightly framed grey hair and sunglasses adorning his head, the friendly proprietor nodded his head as Mitchell extended a greeting in return.

"Well," Mitchell answered promptly, "perhaps one of your local craft beers...yep, let's go with that!"

Mitchell reached for his wallet as he took some cash out to pay for his drink.

"Holiday with the family or here on your own?" the bartender asked nonchalantly as he filled a glass.

"Oh, here with the family," Mitchell responded as he reached for the cold beer, "My congratulatory retirement holiday courtesy of my daughter."

"So, they abandoned you for some shopping pleasure or beach-lounging for the day, eh?" commented the husky-voiced stranger with a light smile.

Mitchell laughed, he sure knew his customers well!

"Traded in for custom designer shoes and artwork I'm afraid!" he answered, still laughing.

"Ah ha, spending your hard-earned retirement dollars, are they?"

"Don't even get me started on that one!" Mitchell laughed.

"Mitchell Fisher of Wilmington, North Carolina." The native Carolinian extended his arm to offer a handshake.

"Walter Kalani, owner of this fine establishment." The gentleman shook Mitchell's hand.

"Pleasure to meet you, Walter!"

Being early afternoon, the riverside bar was modestly filled, giving the proprietor a chance to chat for several minutes with his East Coast patron. Mitchell learned the owner was a native to the island, a retired Army captain.

"After my wife passed," Walter continued with his conversation after a brief pause to provide refreshments to a couple who had taken a seat at the bar, "I decided it was time to hang up the uniform and settle into something...more relaxing. I spent far too many years throwing myself into my work one hundred and ten percent, and I forgot what it was like to relax and enjoy life a little."

"I can relate, I'm a widower myself. I spent many years burying myself into my dental practice." Mitchell shook his head solemnly. "I suppose work was my escape from the reality that Joanna was gone and nothing, not even working twenty-four-seven could fill that void."

"I hear that my friend," Walter replied, leaning on one arm as he pursed his lips together, "there's nothing that can ever substitute for the loss of a loved one."

"I have a beautiful daughter that I am the proud father of, so I do feel blessed. My wife's caregiver also lives with us, Eloise, she has been with us for decades now. She and my wife were quite close, and she stayed on with us after her death to help look after my daughter." Mitchell smiled as he took another swig from his glass. "Drives me absolutely bat-you-know-what crazy sometimes, but I honestly couldn't imagine our lives without her! Any kids yourself?"

Walter nodded his head, "Proud father of two grown sons, both active duty officers in the Army. Followed in their old man's footsteps. I see from your hat you're a veteran yourself."

Mitchell took a quick glance down at his hat, the words U.S Navy were stitched in yellow embroidery across the front.

Mitchell nodded, raising the cap slightly, "Birthday gift from Eloise."

No sooner did he say the words, he felt the vibration of his cell phone in his pocket. Checking the message, he relayed it was, in fact, Eloise wanting to know where he was. Sending back a quick text with his location, he also sent one out to Elizabeth.

Within minutes, Eloise arrived at the bar, bags in hand as she sauntered her way into the establishment. She made herself comfortable at the bar alongside Mitchell as they waited for Elizabeth.

Taking notice of the well-aged bartender conversing with Mitchell, Eloise adjusted her attire as she tried not to stare at the stranger.

Giving Eloise his full attention, his bright eyes twinkled as he smiled.

"On the house ma'am." He wiped his hands politely with a towel before handing her a tiny menu of drink selections.

Turning sideways in her chair to glance at Mitchell, then back at Walter, Eloise coyly responded, "Well now, do you always make it a habit offering free drinks to women who patronize your establishment?"

Walter grinned as he concocted the drink she pointed to on the menu, "Only the ones that catch my undivided attention."

Walter gave Eloise a wink as he handed her the drink.

Caught off guard by his response and beginning to blush, the usually outspoken woman was silent as she sipped on her drink.

"Free drinks and credit cards, you're on quite a roll today!" Mitchell couldn't help but tease his companion. Watching her as she gave him her signature, 'don't go there' glance, she turned her attention back to her admirer.

"Eloise Johnson, a pleasure to make your acquaintance." She put extra emphasis on her name with a slight southern drawl as she extended her hand.

Wiping his hands again with his towel, the friendly bar owner reciprocated, eyes still beaming. "Walter Kalani, very nice to meet you."

Eloise blushed again as Mitchell gave her a sneaky smile.

Breaking the momentary silence, Mitchell inquired with Walter on recommendations for local excursions. Giving the couple some ideas, as he pointed in the air in various directions.

"Hey, guys!" Elizabeth interrupted them as she made her way to the bar.

"Hi, honey, this is Walter. He's been giving us some pointers on what to visit while we're here."

Putting her hand up to offer a brief wave, Elizabeth smiled as she responded to her father's introduction, "I'm Liz, nice to meet you!"

"Care for anything to drink, Liz?" Walter politely asked Elizabeth as she continued leaning against her father, wrapping her arm around his shoulder.

"Oh, I'm okay, thank you," she stated politely, as she declined his offer.

Having finished off their drinks, Mitchell thanked Walter as the trio headed towards the open doorway.

"Oh, Liz, before I forget," Walter called out from behind the bar, "Your father mentioned you were a professional photographer. I highly recommend Aidan up the street. Owns Kapalei Outdoor Excursions, if you're looking for a kayak or trail guide."

"Oh, okay, thank you for the referral. I was planning to find someone who could take me out for a few trips," she replied gratefully.

As they made their way out the door, Eloise took a quick glance over her shoulders. Walter, still watching her, gave her a huge smile.

Embarrassed to have been caught checking him out as they left, Eloise tried to play it off by absently checked her necklace clasp. Smiling in return, she quickened her pace to catch up to Elizabeth and Mitchell.

"You know, I tried to wink at a woman today, and I think it quite nearly got me beat up. He winks and practically gets a standing ovation!" Mitchell wrinkled his nose up as he gave Eloise a smirk.

"What can I say Mitchell, men love me because I'm beautiful!" Eloise shot back with a sassy reply.

Heading back up the road, they passed by the excursion shop recommended by Walter. A ruggedly handsome young man was hoisting a couple of kayaks into a trailer attached to an SUV. Aware he was being watched, he raised his hand up to wave politely.

Eloise wasted no time giving Elizabeth a big, wide-eyed, 'check him out' side glance as she waved back.

Noticing the attractive young man, Elizabeth blushed as she smiled and raised her hand. He smiled back as he continued loading kayaks with another man onto the trailer. Shirtless, his well-toned and tanned torso was clearly visible. Mitchell and Eloise exchanged glances as they all reached the car.

"Bet that was Aidan," Eloise commented, as she looked slyly over her shoulder.

Following her lead, Mitchell added, "Not a bad looking young man!"

"Hmm, I suppose not," she responded as she sheepishly avoided eye contact with either of them.

Good looking was right! She thought to herself. She was certainly going to have to take Walter's recommendation and check Aidan out for herself!

~ * ~

It was late afternoon as the gang arrived back from their town shopping excursion. Mitchell swung the car into the slightly shaded driveway as he glanced back into the rearview mirror, noticing his daughter had stayed surprisingly quiet most the way home.

"Are you doing okay honey?"

"Oh, yeah, I'm fine." Elizabeth nodded her head as she snapped out of her mini-trance. "I think tomorrow I might go down to the kayak shop and see what that guy charges for his outdoor excursions."

Eloise and Mitchell secretly exchanged glances.

"Sure honey, you borrow the car for anything you might feel like doing, I thought I might do a little gardening to keep myself busy, and we know Elle won't need it, she has all her morning soap opera talk shows to watch."

Mitchell gave Eloise a smirk as she stuck her tongue out at him.

"I wanted to get some sunset shots this evening, so I think I will borrow the car now. If I don't get started, I will never get this photo journal done!"

"Sure sweetie, whatever you want," Mitchell answered his daughter as she climbed her way out of the backseat of the two-door vehicle. Mitchell took responsibility for not thinking three people with a two-door car might be inconvenient.

Elizabeth, however, reassured her father she didn't mind climbing in and out of the back seat.

"I'll take Tito with me, give him a chance to breathe the fresh ocean air!"

A few minutes later after Mitchell and Eloise made themselves comfortable in the living room to enjoy their ritual of competitive, evening game shows, Elizabeth made her way with Tito and a black carry bag to the car.

Within ten minutes she reached her destination for the evening.

Taking command of a rocky peninsula overlook stood the simple, yet inviting whitewashed structure of the hundred-year-old Kapalei Lighthouse.

Enjoying a glorious view of the ocean water, Elizabeth inhaled the fresh air as a breeze made its way across the peninsula, tousling her shortly-cropped hair as it passed by. The evening sky began to give way to a beautifully colored sunset. Dotting clouds accented the pink and orange hues like an army of cotton puffs marching across the horizon, or 'cotton balls in the sky' as she often liked to refer them to.

"Pretty spot for some photography work wouldn't you say, little man?" Liz asked her furry companion, engaging him in a one-sided conversation as she often did. The Yorkie wagged his tail as he found a comfortable spot in the grass to plop down.

Getting out a tripod, Elizabeth took her time as she set up her gear.

A day never went by that Elizabeth didn't feel truly grateful for her chosen profession as a freelance photographer.

Allowing her the ability to travel the world doing what she loved most, her career provided a rare pleasure few were fortunate enough to enjoy. Although the pay could be sporadic, her travel expenses were usually covered by her contract employers. Her professional fees afforded her a modest living in New York where she had resided since her mid-twenties.

The evening sky slowly began to give way to a picture-perfect sunset. Her attention returned briefly to the task at hand as she executed several shots, focusing in and out of range to her desired frame. It was only moments before her mind began to wander again, as it often did when she was alone working on a photo shoot.

Elizabeth had originally begun her studies in journalism. After finding herself always feeling out of place in front of a camera, however, she decided to turn her interests into a career behind a camera lens instead.

Having been a studious, but a shy youth, Elizabeth found a comfort zone as she 'hid' behind her first camera at the tender age of twelve, a gift from her father to distract her from the depression she had been carrying after her mother died.

Many days were spent hiding out behind the security of the lens while the growing teen spent her afternoons working on her favorite hobby. Still, Elizabeth continued with a journalism degree. Then, with the help of university professor, she accepted a position with a travel guide firm in her hometown. After a year spent interviewing local restaurants and businesses for the travel magazine, Elizabeth decided to try her hand at professional photography. As her reputation began to build, so did her portfolio and within a few years, she was living in New York working full-time as a freelance photographer.

One benefit of her career choice was the acquaintances she met along the way. They were people she would collaborate with in the industry, and on occasion, she dated a few nice men she met through work. No long-term commitments transpired, however, as marriage and family were never a priority to the independent young woman.

Elizabeth stood still for a moment as she closed her eyes. Focusing on just the light wind caressing her face, she tried not to dwell on the lack of intimate relationships she had partaken in her life. Not that she was prudish but rather, there always lay in the recess of her mind, "If they get attached, and I get sick like mom, would that be fair to someone?" That was the reoccurring question, one of them anyway, that always seemed to gravitate to her mind.

Yes, she would openly admit, living alone and not having strong friendship bonds with any one person, was at times a lonely existence. Elizabeth spent a great deal of time before and after her surgeries seeing counselors that could help her talk out her frustrations, fears, and anxieties. For this reason, she sought out a yoga therapist. She wanted to find someone that not only offered the physical practice but spiritual and meditative guidance as well. More importantly, having been prescribed anti-depressants after her surgeries, the young woman was keen to find a more holistic approach to handling her depression.

Having thoroughly enjoyed her first morning with Gwendoline, or Gwen as she liked to be called, Elizabeth could hardly wait for her next session. She felt confident her new therapist could help her overcome some of the fears she had been harboring since her surgeries.

The memory played over and over in her mind. Elizabeth had been diligently seeing a physician regularly as preventative maintenance. At the ripe age of thirty-three, the young woman, at the advice of her team of doctors, decided to go ahead with the necessary surgeries to reduce her risk of developing the same cancer that killed her mother.

She wasn't, of course, without the support of her father and Eloise. Daily she spoke to Mitchell on the phone, and he made periodic flights up to see her. Eloise, being the mother figure that she was, promptly moved into Elizabeth's tiny apartment, sleeping every night on the sofa, all the while making sure Elizabeth was getting the proper rest and care she needed to recover.

Reaching her hand down to subconsciously rub her abdominal area, she snapped her attention back to the present moment.

Stay in the moment! She reminded herself, a catch-phrase her yoga therapist back in the city would say to her, something she tried to get into the habit of doing whenever she found her mind wandering to dark places.

Elizabeth stood silently as she watched the remaining bits of sun descend upon the ocean's horizon.

Gathering her equipment and Tito's leash, she headed back to the car.

Sitting there briefly, she smiled over at her furry little companion, giving him a gentle scratch behind the ears. As he dutifully licked her fingers, Elizabeth giggled as she leaned over to kiss him on the head.

She had a new adventure planned for the next day, one that she hoped included a certain young man from a certain outdoor excursion shop!

~ * ~

CHAPTER SIX ~ An Outing with Aidan

Leaning over a large fern in the garden, Mitchell noticed a very peculiar sound coming from deep within the vegetation. Sitting up straight while balancing on the back on his heels, he cupped his left ear and listened carefully.

It was mid-morning, and the trio had already indulged in a hearty breakfast. An avid gardener back home, Mitchell found some gardening tools in the garage and set about the task of pruning and familiarizing himself with some of the many native plants adorning the property.

Pausing for a moment, his hat pulled down to protect his eyes from the sun's rays, Mitchell cocked his head to one side, straining to listen for the sound that had caught his attention.

That was a very peculiar sound! He thought to himself. It was a cackling noise proceeded by what sounded oddly enough like someone saying a derogatory word. It continued over and over until it suddenly ceased.

There were no trained parrots hanging about the garden cursing obscenities at him, so he was completely baffled at what he had just heard.

Then suddenly and without warning, Mitchell caught sight of something scurrying across the secluded patio area into the bushes.

What concerned him more than anything was the size of the creature. What on earth was it?

Not one to be fond of creepy critters, Mitchell cautiously made his way towards the bushes. Carrying his spade as though it were a weapon of defense, Mitchell stood amongst the vegetation attempting to peer into them.

As silly as it was, coming from a man who lived in a state where alligators and poisonous snakes lurked about local waterways, he had never warmed up to the idea of anything in his yard that wasn't cute, furry or feathery.

There was complete silence, like the calm before the storm. Then, without warning, a shrill scream could be heard coming from behind Mitchell.

Nearly jumping out of his skin, and dropping his spade to the ground, the poor man swung around to see his daughter and housekeeper standing behind him.

They had noticed his odd behavior from the breakfast room window, and they thought it would be funny to play a joke on him. Knowing her father had weak nerves, Elizabeth and Eloise on more than one occasion had played cruel jokes on him just to get a reaction.

"That was *not* funny you guys!" Mitchell hollered as he put his hand on his chest. Lowering his hands to his hips, he stood there for a moment glaring at them both. Feeling guilty, they both let out a laugh as they apologized.

"Dad, you should have seen yourself."

"Fisher, you looked like you were ready to wage war on a fern bush holding that spade like it was your trusty sword!"

"That's not funny you guys," Mitchell repeated.

"Sorry Dad, we couldn't resist!" Elizabeth approached her father to hug him.

"Honey, I saw something run across the patio, and it wasn't small!" He pointed to the vegetation. "I mean, whatever it was it was huge!"

He held his hands out to demonstrate something that could have been a foot or longer.

"Oh, Dad, I wouldn't worry about it. There's nothing poisonous lurking about here. Besides, are you sure you didn't just see a neighbor's cat run by or something?"

"Well, it's possible. I mean, it was out of the corner of my eye, it could have been a cat. It just made a weird sound, almost, well, almost like it was telling me to go 'eff' myself!"

"You sure that wasn't just the voices in your head again?" Eloise smirked as she made a circular motion with her finger towards her head, insinuating he was crazy.

Mitchell looked as though he was about to raise an offending middle finger at Eloise as she cocked her head sideways giving him another mischievous grin.

Reaching over to push his hand down, playing mediator, as usual, Elizabeth shook her forefinger at her father, giving him the 'no you don't' sign.

"Well, I wouldn't worry about it too much. Just don't leave your bedroom patio door open at night if you're concerned about it." Elizabeth advised.

Spending so many years traveling to countries where the natural habitat was the breeding ground for some truly wondrous, yet creepy, and sometimes dangerous creatures, Elizabeth was no stranger to being cautious of what might lurk in the vicinity. Sometimes, extra precautions had to be taken, so you didn't have uninvited visitors lurking inside your living quarters!

"Now that I'm thinking about it, where's our resident watchdog?" Mitchell scanned the yard, searching for Tito. He had been out in the garden with Mitchell earlier. Did he perhaps see whatever it was and run back in the house, deciding to take sanctuary?

"Last time I checked, he was curled up on my bed for a nap," Elizabeth answered.

The two women headed back inside as Mitchell took one last look at the dense cluster of plants. Deciding that he was done poking around the garden for the day, he thought he would take advantage of the hammock hanging between two trees in the yard, a safe distance from any mystery creature lurking in the garden!

Mitchell picked up his newspaper as he headed over to the hammock, enjoying its vantage point of the scenic overlook down a hillside to the ocean.

Back inside the house, Elizabeth dropped the car keys from the foyer table into one of the pockets of her cargo pants. Comfortable in just a tank top with her favorite headscarf on, she grabbed her sunglasses off the hall table as she bid them both a farewell for the morning. She then gathered up her backpack, which doubled as a camera and tripod carrying case.

"I'll see you guys later," she hollered out. Mitchell, engrossed in his newspaper as he swung casually in the hammock outside, raised a hand up to wave goodbye.

Glancing up briefly from the computer screen, Eloise replied, "Liz, honey, will you do me a favor. Swing by that little church we saw on Main Street and get their hours for me. I'd like to make service this week."

"Sure, not a problem!"

"If the good Lord doesn't stop working his miracles to take a holiday, the least I can do is give him thanks for providing us with one," she spoke loud enough for Mitchell to hear her, "Besides, Fisher may wanna go with me. You know, to give thanks for not being eaten by the dinosaur lurking in his fern plants!"

"Yeah, yeah, I hear ya!" A muffled answer emanated from the backyard.

Elizabeth smiled as she headed out to the car. Feeling a bit anxious, she started the engine and drove down the street towards town as she thought to herself, since when do you get nervous being around some guy?

She shook off the notion as she approached the church. Parking the car in front of a quaint, wooden structure, she noticed how well kept the building and the pretty garden appeared. A colorful array of flowers could be found neatly planted around the church's foundation, with several more clustered along the sidewalk.

Elizabeth slowly meandered her way up the walking path, admiring the gorgeous floral assortment, and watching as a cluster of bees worked to collect pollen from the budding flowers. Reaching the church's front doors, she read the services bulletin board for the information Eloise had requested. She quickly noticed one name that stood out.

Getting out her phone, she sent a text to Eloise with the times, adding an additional message, "I think you are going to *really* enjoy the service!"

Eloise texted back a thank you, oblivious to the clue that was sent. Figuring she would find out for herself, Elizabeth giggled as she headed back to the car.

Pausing for a moment, she decided not to bother moving the car, as she could see the kayak shop from where she was standing.

The young woman retrieved her bag, locked the car, and took a deep breath. She had already formulated a plan so that it wouldn't be a big deal if Aidan were already tied up for the day. She could always make her way over to one of the wilderness reserves for a hike and just enjoy some time for herself.

Making her way inside the ample building, she noticed the shop was filled with all sorts of outdoor activity gear. Everything from camping equipment to clothing hung neatly in rows, available for sale. Through another doorway, one could see an open room with surfboards, paddleboards, and kayaks carefully mounted on adjustable racks. Wetsuits and other safety attire were meticulously hung nearby.

Just as she turned to leave the room, a stocky young man came out from behind two swinging doors.

"Hi there, I'm John, can I help you with anything?" he asked politely.

"Um, well, yes…yes you can," Elizabeth stammered for a moment.

"Walter down at the riverside bar recommended I ask for Aidan, about some guided tours?" she phrased it in a question rather than a statement.

"Oh sure, I'll get him for you."

The young man disappeared behind the swinging doors.

Within moments he was back, followed by the man Elizabeth had waved to the day before.

"Hi, I'm Aidan." The handsome stranger approached Elizabeth from the back room. Noticing an Irish accent immediately, the young woman blushed.

"Um…hi, I'm Liz. Walter recommended I see you about some outdoor guided tours. I was hoping maybe you could tell me what you offer?"

Elizabeth's petite frame dwarfed in comparison to the Irishman's well-toned physique. Wearing a tee shirt, a pair of military-style shorts, and hiking shoes, Aidan slid down onto a stool next to the cash register. He offered her a seat on the other stool next to him, which Elizabeth accepted as she dropped her bag to the floor.

"I'm a photographer by trade, and I want to have someone help show me around to some locations that I could use for a photo journal…well, book, I'm working on," she stuttered as she tried to explain herself.

"Oh, that's cool!" he answered back, seeming impressed. As he gave her a genuine smile, the sides of his greyish-colored eyes crinkled.

Elizabeth couldn't help but notice a slight flutter in her chest. She always did have a weakness for a man with a cute Irish brogue!

"Well, you're in luck." Aidan stood up as he reached behind the counter for a pair of sunglasses and car keys. "I had a couple just cancel on me. Apparently, the wife had a *few* too many fruity, alcoholic beverages last night and is need of recovery this morning, if you know what I mean!"

Aidan grinned as he pointed to his mouth, given indications that the woman was suffering the repercussions of a serious hangover.

Elizabeth laughed. Not only was he cute, but he had a sly sense of humor to boot!

"Well, I guess I'm glad I don't drink then," she responded.

"That makes two of us. I've had more than my fair share of people acting rather surprised that I don't indulge."

"Yeah, I guess because you're Irish, they just assume it."

"Well, being Irish doesn't automatically mean you're born with a stout beer in one hand, and a four-leaf clover in the other. I tell people I prefer to leave the partying to a little wee drunk man in a green suit, running about looking for his rainbow and pot o' gold!"

"With his four-leaf clover in hand, of course." Elizabeth giggled.

"Exactly!" Aidan replied, leading Elizabeth to the door. "I can't say I've ever seen a four-leaf clover in all my life, and I'm yet to find that darn little man to lead me to his vast treasure trove of gold!"

Elizabeth couldn't help but giggle again like a schoolgirl, clearly taken with the friendly Irishman's wit and humor.

Leading her to an open-topped sports utility vehicle hitched to a trailer with three kayaks on it, Aidan excused himself for a moment as he unloaded one of the kayaks and propped it against the building.

Climbing into the vehicle, they secured their seat belts, and the young man navigated the truck in the direction of the majestic cliffs overlooking the ocean.

Having decided to take his client on a kayak tour around Kapalei Bay then up the Na Pali coast, he continued down the road to the boat dock a few miles ahead.

Elizabeth listened intently as Aidan pointed out several spots along Main Street, giving her advice on where to get the best cup of coffee in town and where to find their local farmer's market.

Glancing over at her guide as they drove along, Elizabeth couldn't help but blush again. He sure was a sight to behold to any warm-blooded female!

Short, ginger-brown tresses strayed haphazardly on his head, an obvious sign that the Irishman didn't give too much thought to his styling habits. His facial hair, however, did command some thoughtful attention as he sported a neatly trimmed beard that he would often, and perhaps unconsciously stroke, Elizabeth observed.

"Here we are!" Aidan swung the vehicle into a large parking lot and strategically backed into a spot close to a boating dock. Unloading the kayaks and carrying them down to a sandy area by the shoreline, he made a couple of trips back to the vehicle. Grabbing a bag of gear and two life vests, he motioned to his companion to follow as they made their way down to the kayaks.

"It's a good day to go out, the water's calm, so I can take you over to an area I think you will like to photograph." Aidan handed Elizabeth her life vest as he carefully held the kayak for her to climb in.

Settling himself into his watercraft, Aidan led Elizabeth through the water as the two began the arduous task of paddling away from the beach. Staying close to the shoreline, they slowly paddled along, allowing Elizabeth to sightsee as she took in the amazing views.

The monstrous cliffs extended thousands of feet into the air, and were draped in flora and fauna of all types, making a stunning visual!

Her camera gear already out and prepped, Elizabeth took several photographs as they glided along.

"I'm sure you've seen some stunning places in your line of work," Aidan called over as he maneuvered his kayak closer to Elizabeth's.

She lowered her camera to her lap, as she turned to look in his direction. "I've been pretty lucky, that's for sure. I love what I do, and it's allowed me to see some beautiful places."

"Have you been to Ireland before?"

"I have, I did some work there twice, and absolutely loved it! Whereabouts are you from?" she asked her companion, curious to know more about him.

"Well, I could start from the beginning. My mom's American, from California. Met my dad while he was on holiday with his parents. My grandparents ran a restaurant, where she worked as a teenager. One evening he was there with his parents, and she was smitten with him from the get-go. I suppose she couldn't resist his chiseled good looks and Irish accent!" Aidan smiled as he winked at Elizabeth.

"Anyway, he went home to Dublin, and they wrote each other constantly. A year later, when my mother finished school at the tender age of eighteen, she boarded a plane and headed to Ireland. They married, but sadly, it wasn't meant to be. Trying to raise three small kids while my father worked a blue-collar job meant money was always tight. Coupled with the fact that he had a problem with drinking, she often spent nights going to bed alone and waking up with either a husband that was passed out or not home at all."

Aidan swung the kayak around, as he pointed to a pod of dolphins swimming in the distance. They watched for a few moments as the graceful creatures skimmed the surface of the water. Enjoying the show, Elizabeth took the opportunity to snap several more shots as she continued to listen intently.

"So, you guys didn't stay in Ireland, then?"

"No, I suppose the only thing I have left to attach myself to my native homeland is a slight Irish accent and the Donovan name."

"Was it hard for you all to adjust in the States?"

"No, not really. I have dual citizenship, and I was old enough by then to see the misery my parents were struggling through. Also, I think my mother just wanted the comfort of her own family. She moved my two younger sisters and me back to California. My grandparents helped raise us, and my mom eventually took over running the restaurant. My grandad still stays actively involved with it. Both of my sisters stayed close by. One's married with children of her own and my youngest sister, who's still single like myself, runs the bar at the restaurant."

Elizabeth took note on the emphasis he put on his last comment. Was that a hint? Did he mention being single for a reason?

One could only hope!

"Did she ever remarry?"

"No, she didn't. I don't think she ever truly got over the divorce and I know she never stopped loving my dad. He did remarry eventually. I have two half-brothers, and he's still married to this day. She's a nice woman, and I reckon she had a better grasp on how to handle my father then my mom did."

"Do you ever see him?"

"On occasion, yeah. My younger sister and I flew out there a few years ago to see him, and my other sister and her family went out about a year ago for a visit. He always did well to stay in touch the best he could. I don't harbor any resentment. My family in California, we're close, and my grandparents did more than we could have ever wished for making sure we were loved and happy. My mom, too."

"I notice you say 'mom' and not like, mum or ma?" Elizabeth almost without thinking, blurted it out. "Sorry, that was a dumb question!" She rolled her eyes, as she felt embarrassed that she would even ask something so trivial.

"No, not at all! We left Ireland when I young enough to start picking up the American lingo. I sort of have this hybrid language all of my own, I suppose you could say."

Aidan laughed as he noticed Elizabeth was still blushing.

"I still refer to my grandmother as Granny, and I suppose a word here and there from my Dublin childhood creeps out on occasion." The young man smiled as he unconsciously stroked his facial scruff.

"So, you decided not to pursue the restaurant business then?" She continued to ask more questions, wanting to know as much as possible about the handsome stranger.

He laughed as he tilted his head back slightly, squinting his eyes in the bright sun.

"Ah, yeah," he answered with a slight hint of embarrassment in his response, "I'm afraid my family was a bit hard-pressed to keep me interested in the running the restaurant. I mean, I worked afternoons and weekends helping while I was in school. I suppose I just had more interest in spending my time outdoors, surfing and camping...things like that."

He paused as he took a drink of water. "I studied marine biology at a local university, but it's a highly competitive field to find work. After a few more years helping at the restaurant, one thing led to another, and I found myself living in Maui working as an adventure guide instead. I had a buddy here in Kauai, and the opportunity presented itself to take over his business when he went back to the mainland. I've been here ever since!"

Elizabeth smiled as she watched Aidan guide them around a long bend into a cove.

"Check this out!" He pointed ahead to a natural waterfall inside the cove. The awe-inspiring scene was breathtaking! They slowly paddled in closer as Elizabeth took several close-range photos.

"Do you mind?" she asked politely, as she handed the camera to him.

"No, not at all!" Aidan reached for the camera as she paddled closer to the waterfall, positioning herself just in front of it.

"I'm a bit prehistoric when it comes to fancy technology," he hollered out as he inspected the complicated camera.

"No worries! It's set to take the photos in autofocus. Go ahead and just push the button," she instructed as he looked down at the digital screen.

"Got it!" Aidan called out as he took a couple of shots of her. "Now pump your fists in the air like you just conquered the biggest feat in your life!"

Elizabeth laughed. The shy young woman did as she was told, spreading her arms out and, following Aidan's lead, giving a war cry.

"There ya go!" he said while giving her two thumbs up as she paddled back to his side.

Elizabeth smiled politely as she reached out for her camera. It was the first time in a long while that she felt excited about doing something socially with someone new. She was looking forward to enjoying his company again.

"Well, I don't want you to be too tired, so we're going to head back if that's alright with you?"

"Oh, that's fine. I promised my family I would be back in the afternoon so we could all do something together.

"Well, missy, since I just divulged my life's history, I think it's only fair you tell me more about yourself!" Aidan grinned as he glanced over at his companion.

"Oh gosh," Elizabeth started, hesitating a bit. "There's not much to tell really."

"Everybody has a backstory!"

"Well, I live in New York, I have a little studio there. I am gone a lot with my job, but I love being able to travel as much as I do. I have a ten-year-old Yorkie named Tito, who fortunately travels with me frequently. If I know I'm going to be gone a few weeks or more somewhere that it would be more hassle to bring him, he stays with my dad and our housekeeper in North Carolina, so he doesn't have to be stuck in a boarding facility."

She stopped momentarily to take a drink of water. Keeping up a consistent pace, you needed the upper body strength for all the paddling! In all fairness to her guide, he had asked her what her physical comfort level was and how much experience she had. He tried to cater his tours to the activity level that was safe and comfortable for his clients.

"I'm close with my Dad and Eloise. She was my mom's caregiver years ago. My mom died when I was ten from cancer, and she's lived with us ever since. Honestly, my father would be completely useless around the house if it wasn't for Elle."

"I'm sorry about your mother." Aidan's response touched her. She smiled as she took a deep breath, trying not to get emotional about it. There were days where she could think about her mom and just reflect on the good times. Then, there were the days where the loss of her mother seemed like yesterday, and she would tear up thinking about her.

"Eloise is our rock. She's hilarious, I mean, she keeps my dad on his toes. It was like having a mom and a cool big sister around at the same time."

Selectively, Elizabeth decided not to talk too much about herself. She did after all, just meet this guy. He didn't need to know that she battled with severe depression, she could never have children and had been without a real boyfriend for years.

Something instinctively told her that it wouldn't matter if he did know. Elizabeth got the impression that he was different. Someone you could open up to and tell him whatever you were thinking. He had that aura about him.

The pair made small talk as they continued back to shore. Elizabeth was quick to change the subject and ask Aidan more questions about himself. They had quite a lot in common, she had thought to herself. He said he was often a loner, and spent much of his free time just camping or hanging out at home playing his guitar when he wasn't busy with work.

Thirty minutes later they found themselves back in town and approaching the shop.

Once inside, Elizabeth fished into her waterproof bag as she unzipped a compartment to give Aidan her credit card.

"Don't worry about today. It's on the house." The young man smiled as he leaned against the doorframe leading to the back of the shop.

"No, I insist. How do you expect to run a business if you don't take payment for your time?"

"You're beginning to sound like my grandad!" He laughed as he refused to take the card, his hands still in his pockets. Biting slightly on his lip, he continued to watch Elizabeth as she reluctantly put the credit card back in her bag.

"Okay, well, just this time. I know my father would like the waterfall excursion. I could get some great photographs there, and I'd like to do the trail hike you offer as well."

"The day hike or the overnight camp out?"

"Um, well, it might be kind of cool to do the overnight camping one," she answered almost timidly, realizing that she was probably blushing profusely at that very moment.

Thanking him again for the excursion, she made her way back to the car, all the while replaying the day's events in mind.

She sure was looking forward to her next adventure out!

~ * ~

CHAPTER SEVEN ~ Legend of Tokay Stalker

A few days had past, and it was late afternoon when Elizabeth arrived back to the house from her yoga session for the day. Deciding not to go into town to one of the busier restaurants, Mitchell booked reservations at one of the resorts for a luau dinner overlooking the ocean instead.

Waiting for the girls to finish getting ready, he made his way out to the bench swing opposite the kitchen patio. Sitting down to enjoy the late afternoon breeze, Mitchell pushed the swing along as he relaxed. The fragrance from the various floral plants sweetened the air as he closed his eyes momentarily, taking in several deeps breaths.

Mitchell opened his eyes after his moment of solitude. Watching as Tito made himself a comfortable sitting spot in the grass near the swing, he observed the little dog's behavior suddenly change.

His ears perked up, the Yorkie sat very still as he scanned the garden. A low growling noise could be heard coming from the dog's throat as he suddenly jumped up and ran back to the house, squeezing himself through the patio door, which Mitchell had left slightly open him.

Slowing down the swing, Mitchell stopped it altogether. Sitting still, he strained to hear something, anything, that may have aggravated the dog.

Within moments a low, almost barking sound could be heard coming from deep within the vegetation. Determined to find the cause of the odd noise, Mitchell carefully made his way into the mixture of ferns and flower bushes. Trying to keep his dinner attire clean, he slowly weaved his way in and around the various plants until he found himself standing in the middle of the garden bed.

Kneeling to take a better look within the vegetation, Mitchell continued to strain his ears and listen.

Completely absorbed with his task at hand, Mitchell was oblivious to his daughter, who had walked out to the patio's edge.

"DAD, we've been calling for you!" Elizabeth hollered at the top of her lungs.

Jumping up suddenly, Mitchell did not take notice that he had, in fact, wandered under a tree.

Turning around and stepping forward simultaneously, Mitchell walked smack center into a low-level branch. Hearing the loud cracking sound, he instantly felt a dull throbbing in his forehead.

Then suddenly, as if in slow motion, he tumbled backward into a cluster of ferns. Like a heavy sack of potatoes, Mitchell felt the weight of his body collapse to the ground.

Lying there for what seemed an eternity, Mitchell blinked his eyes several times. The faint, muffled sound of his daughter yelling for Eloise could be heard coming from the yard. Lying still, Mitchell focused on the rays of the sun he could see shimmering down on him through the trees.

Then, without warning, Mitchell felt something climb across his leg. Still unable to move his body, a feeling of fear began to wash over him.

82

What the heck was crawling on his leg? Worse yet, what if it was something poisonous? Were there deadly animals in Kauai? The questions penetrated Mitchell's mind as his head throbbed with pain. He never thought to check the travel guides for potentially lethal animals that might lurk in one's garden!

Trying not to panic, Mitchell stayed as still as possible. Isn't that what they teach you in outdoor survival classes? Not to make any sudden moves?

Still unable lift his head to see what was clambering across his leg, he felt the steady movement of claws digging down into his shins.

Out of the corner of his eye, he saw Elizabeth and Eloise hurriedly trying to weave their way through the dense vegetation.

Whatever it was, it was certainly big enough! He thought to himself, as he could feel two pairs of claws, one on each leg. As his daughter made her way through the cluster of plants, the creature made a mad dash for cover, not before Mitchell felt the thick underside of its entire body slither across both his legs.

"Dad, oh my God, are you okay?"

"Mitchell, don't move, you might have broken something!" Eloise knelt next to the fallen man and leaned forward to check the extent of his forehead injury.

"Well, you have a nasty bump there Mitchell, but thankfully you're not bleeding. Can you feel your fingers and toes?"

He slowly began moving his limbs. Feeling achy but able to move, Mitchell attempted to sit up.

"Uh, Dad, I don't think you should try and move. You may have a concussion or neck injury." Elizabeth put her hand out as though she were trying to keep her father from getting up.

"Honey, I'm fine really. A little dizzy, but I can feel all my limbs."

"Mitchell, she's right, you might have a severe injury we can't see. I'm going to call for an ambulance."

Eloise hurriedly made her way back to the house, climbing over several plants in the process. Liz turned her attention back to her father.

"What on earth were you doing climbing into the bushes?"

"I'd rather not get into it, to be honest," Mitchell stated, already feeling his wounded pride.

"Okay, well…if it was that animal you thought you saw before, I don't see anything lurking around." Elizabeth made a point to sit up on her knees as she strained to look around the garden for anything suspicious.

Returning with her cell phone in hand, Eloise crouched down next to Mitchell, "They're on their way now, don't try and move."

Within minutes a siren could be heard as an emergency transport vehicle pulled into the driveway. Eloise headed across the lawn and was joined by two emergency medical technicians.

"Um, Dad, try not to cringe okay?"

"Why do you say that, honey?"

As Mitchell attempted to glance over at the figures making their way through the shrubbery, a familiar voice could be heard.

"Well, Mr. Fisher," the sound of a deep voice could be heard, "we meet again!"

A large and looming shadow blocked the sun's rays from Mitchell's eyes as he stared face to face with Officer Kahele.

"I'm okay, Officer Kahele." Mitchell attempted to sit up.

"Today it's EMT Kahele, Mr. Fisher." The emergency technician rested his hand on Mitchell's chest, discouraging him from trying to sit up. "I provide my services and skill set as a first responder on weekends to assist our fine community."

Elizabeth and Eloise glanced at each as they attempted not to snicker at the seriousness in the man's voice.

"What exactly brought you into the bushes in the first place Mr. Fisher?"

"I'd rather not say."

Eloise rolled her eyes as she interjected herself, as usual, into the conversation.

"Mitchell thinks he's being stalked by some creature living in our bushes. Last time he heard it, he swore it was telling him to go 'eff' himself!"

"Hum, interesting." Kahele's brown eyes narrowed slightly.

"Are you on medication, Mr. Fisher?"

"No, I'm not taking any medications." Mitchell, exasperated by the attention, was feeling frustrated by the whole ordeal.

"Have you been drinking?"

"I don't drink. Well, a beer now and then, and I don't do illegal narcotics. About the worst thing I've ever done was inadvertently smuggle illegal apples through customs!"

85

"I see you haven't lost your sense of humor, Mr. Fisher." Kahele kneeled over Mitchell as he and his partner hoisted the man onto a backboard. Strapping him down, they proceeded to carry him around to the ambulance parked in the driveway.

Elizabeth climbed into the back of the ambulance while Eloise followed in the car. After a thorough checkup, it was determined that Mitchell would be okay, having suffered just a slight concussion. Releasing him to go home, the trio made their way back to the house.

"I'm sorry I ruined our evening out, girls."

"Don't worry about that. We're just glad you're okay."

"Thankfully, you're not seriously hurt, and the swelling will go down soon enough!" Eloise glanced over from the driver's side of the vehicle as she grinned at Mitchell.

"Thank you, girls, I appreciate you deciding it was important enough have me checked out, just to be on the safe side." Mitchell adjusted the oversized sunhat he had left sitting in the backseat of the car as they slowly made their way back to the house.

"If I didn't know any better, I would swear Agent, Officer, err, EMT whatever his name is...Kahele, was laughing to himself!" Mitchell wrinkled his nose as he reflected back on the incident.

"Oh, don't be silly Dad, he has no reason to do that!"

"I'm just sorry I ruined the luau!"

"Another time, Mitchell," said Eloise, "I can put something together for us here at the house. If you're feeling better, perhaps tomorrow you'll accompany me to church so that we can give thanks to the good Lord you didn't knock yourself clean out!"

~ * ~

Later that evening, after everyone had long gone to bed, Mitchell heard a faint scratching at the door leading out to the patio.

Slowly propping up on one arm, Mitchell instinctively raised his hand to his forehead. Feeling a large bump, he cringed as he recapped the afternoon's event.

Hearing a slight whimper, he forced himself to sit upright. Still groggy from sleep and the pain medication the hospital gave him, Mitchell opened one eye as he stumbled out of bed.

Shuffling across the floor, Mitchell saw Tito sitting next to the sliding glass door.

"Got to do your business buddy?"

Tito pawed at the door as Mitchell, still half asleep, unlocked the patio door and slid it open a few inches. He stood there swaying back and forth from the grogginess as Tito meandered onto the porch.

Waiting several minutes while Tito sniffed around the yard, Mitchell turned to head back to his bed.

"Let yourself back in will ya little guy," he instructed the dog as he wandered back to his bed. Within minutes of his head resting on his pillow, Mitchell was soundly snoring away.

Meanwhile, Tito wandered towards the bushes where Mitchell had his unfortunate accident only hours before. Sniffing the ground feverishly, he stopped suddenly.

Tito's ears perked up as something deep within the vegetation caught his attention. He growled as the dark shadow of something pacing near the plants began to make a steady dash in his direction. A loud hissing could be heard as the creature swiftly advanced towards the dog.

Not wanting to hang around and find out what was lurking in the garden, the little dog squealed as he ran back towards the house. Squeezing his way through the open door, Tito ran past Mitchell's bed and out through the half-opened bedroom door, down the hall to Elizabeth's room.

Snoring loudly, Mitchell was unaware the dog had returned to the house, with the patio door still left unattended.

He was also unaware that whatever had been lurking in the bushes that frightened Tito was now creeping its way across his bedroom floor.

~ * ~

"Tito, will you please stop crawling on my chest, you weigh a ton!" Mitchell shifted his body back and forth as he awoke to the feeling of fresh air blowing across his face.

Blinking his eyes several times to adjust to the morning light filtering its way through the closed window blinds, Mitchell reached his hand up to rub his unshaven face.

Glancing down at his bedspread to see a large mound slowly moving closer to his face, he chuckled to himself.

It wasn't unlike the terrier to crawl under the covers to cuddle up next to someone at night to sleep, but unusual for him to climb over one's chest.

"Tito, seriously, that tickles." Mitchell glanced down again at the bulge under the cover.

Then he heard a light whimper next to the bed. Turning his head to the left, he saw Tito pawing at the blankets as he began to bark incessantly.

"Oh, no." Mitchell looked at the foot of his bed as he saw the patio door had been left open. "Geez, you have got to be kidding me!"

Mitchell, now alert, came to the full realization that whatever was crawling slowly up his body, was not, in fact, his daughter's dog.

A throaty barking sound could be heard emanating from under the bedspread. Two sets of claws could be felt pressing themselves through Mitchell's flannel sleepwear, and what felt like a long tail was swaying back and forth across his gut.

Deciding not to waste any more time dreading the inevitable, he reached down, gripping the cover as he flung it back as far as he could.

Mitchell's eyes grew wide as he was now face to face with the largest reptile he had ever encountered!

Measuring a good twelve inches or more, the lizard continued to bounce up and down on Mitchell's chest, hissing loudly, it's green eyes dilated. It's vibrant blue and orange skin made for an interesting contrast to Mitchell's plaid flannel attire.

"Mitchell, how ya feeling this morning?" Eloise could be heard calling down the hallway, oblivious to the precarious situation going on in his bedroom.

"Do you think you feel up to…Oh, my word!" Eloise shrieked as she opened the bedroom door, stopping dead in her tracks.

"I have no idea what in the heck it is, but will you please…get…it…off…me!" Mitchell tried to remain calm as the highly agitated creature opened its mouth wide, as though prepared to bite.

"What do you mean, get it off you? I'm not touching that thing! It's like two feet long, and oh, my good God does it look pissed!"

"Please, go get Liz!" Mitchell tried to whisper, all the while trying not to look the large reptile in the eye.

"I'm going, I'm going!"

Eloise went running down the hall hollering Elizabeth's name as Tito continued to bark at the commotion on the bed.

"Shut up Tito. You are not helping the situation!"

Within moments, Elizabeth appeared at the bedroom door, still dressed in her pajamas, as she tucked her disheveled hair behind her ears.

"There is a very large and very angry lizard sitting on your father's head!" Eloise could be heard exaggerating the circumstances as she stood behind Elizabeth.

"Is this thing going to bite me?" Mitchell asked softly as his daughter stood in the doorway of the room, shocked at the scene she was witnessing.

"Um, Dad, don't make any sudden moves."

"What in the heck is that thing?" Eloise asked as she continued to peer over Elizabeth's shoulder.

Elizabeth couldn't help but let out a slightly nervous giggle. "It's a gecko."

"A gecko? That is *not* a gecko! Geckoes are tiny, cute and talk with a British accent. That is something out of a horror movie!" Eloise's eyes grew wide as Elizabeth walked to the side of the bed and almost nonchalantly scooped the creature up, keeping a firm grip on his body, so he wasn't inclined to turn his head and bite her.

"Yeah guys, he's a tokay gecko. They aren't native to Hawaii, you normally find them in Asia. I've seen loads of them. You just need to know how to handle them, and if they're agitated, leave them alone. They are known to have a wicked bite!"

"Where are you putting that thing, Elizabeth?" Her father demanded to know.

"Back in the garden where he belongs."

"Isn't there some animal control we can call to come collect it. I mean, what if it got back in the house again?"

Elizabeth stopped for a moment, as she had begun to step onto the outside patio.

"This is *your* habitat in here," she stated firmly as she motioned her head in the air referring to the interior of the house, "and that is *his* habitat out there." She nodded her head in the direction of the garden. "We can't just relocate him because you don't like the thought of him being in the yard. He could have a mate, and he's got to feed so he needs to be left where we found him."

Elizabeth, stating her case, refused to be swayed. Ignoring her father's plea, she headed out of the house and into the garden. Setting the lizard down on the ground, she watched as it scurried its way back into the brush.

Heading back into her father's bedroom, the young woman stepped into the adjacent bathroom and washed her hands.

"Okay, done deal. Keep your door closed at night, I told you that!" Elizabeth reprimanded her father as he sat in bed, rolling his eyes as his daughter's scolding.

Eloise could be heard laughing from the corner of the room. "You should have seen your face, Mitchell Fisher, Lord have mercy!"

"That's not funny, Elle!" Mitchell flung his legs over the side of the bed, while he continued to rub his bumpy forehead.

"Dad, go to church with Eloise. It will make you feel better to get out and get some fresh air."

"I think that may be a good idea, honey, thank you."

"You can pray for thanks that you still have your nose intact!" Eloise quipped as she left the room heading into the hallway.

"Looks like you could write a book about this one. The Legend of the Tokay Stalker!" Reaching down to scoop Tito up in her arms, Elizabeth couldn't help but giggle at her own joke.

Mitchell stood as he gave his daughter a quick kiss on the forehead, thanking her for her help before making his way to the suite's bathroom.

He leaned over the bathroom sink as he splashed cool water on his face. Inspecting the large bump that had formed on his head, he rolled his eyes as he tidied himself up.

What a way to start your first week of retirement holiday! Mitchell recapped the week's events from the time they left the East Coast to the present moment.

He almost had to question whether coming to the island had been a good idea or not.

Mitchell just couldn't quite shake the nagging feeling of uncertainty that continued to linger somewhere deep inside.

~ * ~

CHAPTER EIGHT ~ Ocean Therapy

After the craziness of the morning drama, Mitchell was thoroughly relieved to get away from the house and get some fresh air.

With the convertible top down, Eloise informed Mitchell she would be doing the driving that morning, as he needed to give his eyes and mind a break from any strenuous activity.

Making sure he had his hat with him, partially for vanity to cover up the massive lump on his forehead, he made himself comfortable as they headed down the road.

"I do believe our Elizabeth may just be a bit smitten with that local guide, do you think?" Mitchell asked Eloise as he chuckled lightly, striking up a conversation about a topic not related to their earlier drama.

He was all too aware of his daughter's lack of interest in the opposite sex since her surgeries. He was compassionate enough to understand that she simply wasn't ready to make any commitments to a relationship, given the sensitive nature of her health.

"Well, the child has to get out there and live life! Staying cooped up all day in her flat or shutting herself off from socializing when she works isn't going to help. She needs to get past this stigma she's created in her head, that she can't meet someone and have a loving relationship." Eloise shook her head as she slowed down to yield a safety light.

"Honestly Elle, who are we to talk? I mean really, neither of us have been out in the dating field, in like what, five hundred years?"

Eloise couldn't help but laugh at the reality of his comment. It was true, they both had, in fact, stayed single since their spouses had passed away. Eloise had tried dating a few men she met over the years, but nothing panned out long term as she found herself comfortable in her life at the Fisher's homestead. Besides, she had always felt herself comparing each date to her late husband, a habit she was never able to refrain from.

Mitchell, for his part, was resigned to knowing that no one would ever fill the void left by Joanna. Instead, he had focused his life on his career and daughter.

The two arrived shortly before the service began as they made their way into the bustling little church. Wandering down the aisle to a pew closest to the minister's pulpit, they were greeted by warm and friendly locals and fellow tourists alike.

Mitchell and Eloise exchanged pleasantries with other patrons of the church, completely unaware of the minister making his way up the aisle greeting his congregation.

"Well, good morning and thank you for joining us today!" A familiar voice could be heard approaching the couple as they turned to face Walter, the tiki bar owner.

Unable to hide her surprise, Eloise blushed as she turned to give Mitchell a quick glance.

Mitchell, grinning wide with amusement, extended his hand. "Fancy seeing you here this morning, Walter. I see you will be engaging us in our morning worship!"

Smartly dressed in black slacks and a crisp white shirt, Walter beamed with a friendly smile as he gave Eloise a quick wink.

Nonchalantly brushing her hand across her long and flowing, floral-printed summer dress, Eloise nodded her head politely as she clutched a leather-bound book tightly to her chest with her other hand.

"I see we do double duty as local bar owner by night and town preacher by day?" She coyly stated as she found herself beguiled by the charismatic man. Ironically enough, having had the thoughts not but fifteen minutes earlier on why she wasn't interested in dating, she couldn't help but entertain the notion that Walter was different. Like a kindred spirit of some kind.

"I do indeed! I fill in on occasion for our resident minister, who is most unfortunately laid up the next few weeks recovering from a rotator cuff injury." Walter quietly replied as several more parishioners made their way past the trio to their seats. Leaning in to whisper, "I believe a strenuous day on the golf course was deemed the guilty party!"

Mitchell and Eloise laughed, as no one ever said a round of golf wasn't without its vices!

Making his way to the pulpit, Eloise continued to feel her cheeks flush as she watched the handsome older gentleman engage the standing choir in song.

"Let me guess, and he keeps a fully stocked fridge in the back for emergencies?" Mitchell leaned over to whisper in Eloise's ear as they took their seats. Giving him a disapproving jab with her elbow, she pursed her lips together indicating she did not find his joke funny.

"We are in the house of the Lord, Mitchell, do remember that!"

Still snickering at his joke, Mitchell smugly returned his attention to the choir that had begun to sing. Standing to join them in song, Mitchell removed the hat he had been wearing to hide his still visible head injury.

Leaning over to whisper into Mitchell's ear, Eloise made sure to have the last word. "Pray the good Lord heals that hideous lump on your forehead Mitchell, we wouldn't want you scaring small children or anything!"

Returning the jab of the elbow, Mitchell gently shoved Eloise as she snickered to herself.

Two hours later, after the service had drawn to a close, Mitchell and Eloise began to shuttle their way down the aisle amongst their fellow churchgoers.

"Eloise, Mitchell, if you have a moment?" They heard the husky voice call out from behind.

Walter quickly maneuvered his way towards the couple as they had begun to make their way out of the church.

Staring intently at Eloise, Walter cleared his throat as he held the door open for her.

"I was wondering if perhaps you, the both of you," he was sure to glance at Mitchell, so he felt included in the conversation, "would be interested in dinner down at the resort Monday night? It's usually slow the early part of the week for me at the bar, and my weekend bartender covers the extra hours."

Eloise completely caught off guard, hesitated momentarily. Mitchell, casting a glance over at his companion, was quick to fill the momentary void of silence.

"Well, funny you should ask Walter, we had to cancel a dinner reservation just the other night...sure, we'd love to join you!"

Absently toying with the ornate necklace draped across her neckline, Eloise smiled and seemed at a loss for words.

"Great, I can meet you both there, say, seven o'clock!" Walter beamed as he nodded his head at the pair before turning his attention to a small crowd of the congregation that had been waiting patiently by the church door to garner an audience with him.

As they made their way to their vehicle, Mitchell gave his companion another slight jab with his elbow.

"Time to break that five-hundred-year-old dry spell, ole' girl!"

Still thinking about the sudden offer of dinner, Eloise looked down at her summer dress. Not hitting back at Mitchell with her usual sarcasm, her attention turned to the half a dozen or so clothing shops that lined the town's busy main street.

"I need to find something to wear. I don't know that I brought enough dinner dresses with me."

Mitchell could help but burst out laughing, "You, not have enough outfits to wear? You flew to Hawaii with an entire department store packed in your travel luggage!"

Snapping back to the present moment, Eloise reached over and pinched Mitchell in the arm, causing the man to jump and howl.

"Oh, hush! I need you to drop me off in the morning. I think I recall seeing a salon over near the supermarket. Oh dear, I need to get these nails done!"

Eloise bantered more to herself as they reached their vehicle at the end of the parking lot. Outstretched hands in the air, she carefully inspected her already meticulous fingers.

"Do you think I should do something with my hair?" Mitchell quipped as he pretended to pat on invisible strands of hair.

"What hair, Mitchell Fisher? You are about as bald as a baby's bottom!" Eloise flicked him with her left hand.

"Ah, there's the sarcasm I know and love!"

~ * ~

"Deep inhalation," Gwen instructed the small group of men and women sitting in upright positions with their legs crossed in front of them, "again, focus on your belly movement as you inhale…and release."

Elizabeth sat quietly on her mat as she followed the teacher's instruction. The yogini continued with the breathing exercise as she ended their late morning practice.

"Namaste." Gwen peacefully placed her palms together as she bowed her head to her group.

"Namaste." The group replied in unison.

Opening their eyes, the small group thanked their teacher for the refreshing and enlightening practice. After a few moments of small talk, one by one they trickled off the sandy beach as they left for the day.

Privileged to have a coveted spot on the beach, Gwen had made a genuine oasis for both herself and her clients.

A comfortable private residence was built just yards from the shoreline. A beautifully landscaped garden circled a cluster of palms shading a corner of the property. A smaller, circular structure overlooked the water, as it was used for Gwen's indoor practice if it happened to be a rainy day.

Following her instructor back to the quaint and functional outdoor studio, Elizabeth opened her mat on the tiger-stripe bamboo floor and sat down. Drinking some fresh water from her portable glass container, the young woman stretched her legs out in front of her.

"Thank you, Gwen, for the amazing class!" The young woman gushed as the older woman unrolled a padded mat, covering it with a thin beach blanket.

"Oh, thank you, dear," she responded in a charming British accent. "It's a true pleasure to see clients leave feeling refreshed, energized and happy!"

Her kindly smile radiated as her bright blue eyes sparkled.

The instructor, who appeared to be close to her father's age, casually sat down on her mat.

Snow white hair was neatly tucked behind her ears, bangs softly framing her face. Tall and fit, with a hint of a tan, Gwen was certainly a very attractive woman. Small silver earrings hung daintily from her ears as she readjusted an ornate arm cuff accented with mother-of-pearl.

"Well, love, since this is our first official private session, let me tell you a bit more about myself," she began as she slipped a see-through shawl over her toned shoulders. "I always like to give new clients an introduction, so they know they are working with someone who is very much a regular, normal person with flaws, and how I got to where I am today."

"That sounds good, thank you." Elizabeth politely replied, watching the woman intently.

"Well, I shall begin from the absolute beginning!" Gwen smiled as she spoke for several minutes, filling Elizabeth in on her upbringing and what had brought her halfway around the world from her native England.

Elizabeth learned that Gwen, Gwendolyn Alsop to be exact, had a typically conventional, British upbringing. Growing up attending private boarding schools, the daughter of a banker, Gwen had decided early on she had no desire to marry immediately and become a society wife. She had her own aspirations, and after acquiring her nursing degree, she worked as a volunteer in India. That, she said, was where her love of the yoga practice had begun.

The young woman, overly excited at learning this information couldn't keep to herself that she too, took up yoga while spending three weeks in India on assignment. Both ladies gushed about their travels through the beautiful country. Gwen continued as she explained how she met her former husband, an American practicing medicine at a London hospital where she worked as a nurse.

"Before you could blink an eye, I was madly in love, and we were married less than eight weeks later!" She went on to explain that the newlyweds had decided not to pursue having a family for a while as they both were individually 'married' to their careers.

"We first started coming to Hawaii in the late nineties as we settled on purchasing land, then had the house built. We would commute every year for a few weeks at a time to holiday here on Kauai."

"Then, sadly, the realities of life hit the fan." Gwen took a slow sip from her water bottle. "My husband of twenty-years confessed to me that he was sleeping with a co-worker, half his age, and he wanted a divorce. As if it gets anymore cliché than that!"

The dignified woman rolled her eyes as she shook her head.

"So, I decided now that I was a dual citizen, why stay in London? I had a beautiful home on a tropical island, a philandering ex-husband bound to alimony payments till death do one of us part anyway, why not move here permanently! I had the studio built, and I did some remodeling to the property to accommodate a large parking area. I decided to start my therapeutic practice here in Kapalei, and I haven't looked back since!"

A smile beamed across her face as she looked around the open and airy studio space.

Elizabeth couldn't help but feel an attachment almost immediately to the kindly yogini.

"I have read your intake form thoroughly my dear, so I am very aware of your health status and your family's health history." She went on as her eyes perused a stapled document she had removed from a file folder.

"I see that you underwent a hysterectomy with a bilateral oophorectomy two years ago. Are you currently still under supervision with a follow-up clinic or physician? Are you taking any medications?"

"Yes, I am. My doctor back in New York, Dr. Khan, is my primary physician. He gave me a referral to see Dr. Estrada at the Kapalei Clinic. I need to call their office and schedule an appointment to see him."

Elizabeth paused briefly, aware that she was rubbing her hand lightly over her abdomen.

"I take estrogen therapy pills prescribed for me, to keep everything from getting...um, out of whack I suppose!"

Elizabeth smiled at her therapist for a moment as she reflected on the appointments with her doctors in New York and the reasons they had given her to continue with the medication. "I've also been seeing a doctor for the depression and anxiety I've been suffering with for years. I think the depression was exacerbated after the surgeries."

Gwen gave her client a warm smile as she reached a hand out to pat the young woman's arm gently.

"Miguel is a wonderful doctor Liz, and you will feel very comfortable with him. A genuinely kind and caring man in his field, very professional yet warm with his patients. You will certainly feel like you are getting the adequate care and attention you need. He does not treat his patients like they are just a number for the day. Oh, and I would be lying if I didn't say he's gorgeous to boot!"

Elizabeth laughed, slightly blushing at the same time.

"Sadly, he is just eye candy for us mere mortals, as he is married with two little girls. Still, one can't help but sit and admire that sort of chiseled perfection!" Gwen beamed as she was mentally pictured the man's face while she spoke.

Elizabeth giggled again as she was guilty to jump on the ogle train with Gwen. "I suppose one can look, just not touch!"

"Look, they most certainly can…stare would be a better word!"

"Well, my dear, let's go ahead and have you lie down so we can get started." Gwen stood and had Elizabeth make herself comfortable on the large, padded mat.

Gwen went on to explain that she was still a licensed registered nurse on the island and was very careful in detailing the physical and energy work she was going to do with the young woman. She would also incorporate what they called Thai yoga therapy, which involved stretching to help release tension while being medically cautious regarding where on the young woman's body she would focus her energies.

After an hour of therapy, Elizabeth found herself slowly waking up from what had been a state of semi-consciousness.

"Did I fall asleep?" The young woman asked as she sat up slowly, feeling very relaxed.

"I like to say you allowed your mind, body, and spirit to go to a meditative place for some peaceful, inner contemplation," she replied, smiling as she gently helped Elizabeth to her feet, "with a hint of snoring added to the end for good measure."

"Oh geez, did I start snoring?" Elizabeth asked, blushing from embarrassment.

"I'm pretty sure your snoring was competing with the birds squawking on the rooftop." Gwen teased as she pointed towards the ceiling.

Elizabeth laughed again as she thanked Gwen for the therapeutic hour. They outlined a schedule to meet twice each week for a private session following the morning class.

"On Wednesdays, we do have our Paddleboard class. I highly recommend it. We have the most delightful Irishman who meets with us as he supplies our boards."

Elizabeth bit her lower lip as she blushed again. "That wouldn't happen to be Aidan, would it?" she asked, already knowing the answer.

"Are you in love yet?" Gwen smiled wide as her eyes sparkled, "Is he not the cutest thing you have ever seen? And that darling Irish brogue of his!"

Gwen walked Elizabeth down to her car as they chatted briefly about the young woman's family.

"So, your father has stayed single all these years then?"

"Yeah, he just decided after mom was gone that he would rather be alone than date a lot of women. It never was my father's style."

"That's very admirable of him. His love has stayed loyal to your mother's memory all these years. I very much respect that."

105

"After all this time, I think he might find himself getting lonely and bored. Now all he has is his gardening, fishing and an occasional game of golf. Knowing Eloise, she's going to wish he would get a girlfriend, now that he's going to be home constantly!"

Elizabeth laughed as she contemplated the idea. Knowing them both as well as she did, she knew it was only a matter of time before they would start getting on each other's nerves.

Seeming comfortable with her own sexuality, the genteel woman smiled as she spoke briefly of the few men she had dated since her divorce. In the end, she found living alone to be her comfort zone.

"You can look at being single in two ways. As a lonely existence in life, or a peaceful solitude. I prefer to see it as the latter."

Gwen gave Elizabeth a wink as she held the car door open for the young woman. "Ironically enough, my dear friend Walter sent me a text this morning asking if I'd help him out by joining him on a double date. He was brief, so I frankly have no idea for whom I am to assist in entertaining tomorrow evening. Bless his heart, he hasn't dated in years and I gather a visitor to our fine little island has caught his fancy!"

Gwen gave the young woman a hug as they exchanged goodbyes. Both were unaware that Walter had been referring to Eloise and Mitchell.

Elizabeth contemplated Gwen's statement as she made her way out onto the quiet, tree-lined residential street.

She had never really thought of the independent single life in that way, but it made sense. One could either see it in an optimistic way or pessimistic one. Elizabeth thought to herself, the more positive your mindset, the happier you are in accepting and embracing a single lifestyle!

Elizabeth picked up the pace as glanced at the clock on the car's dashboard. She had promised she would be home in time for an early afternoon luncheon in town.

She smiled to herself as she recalled the conversation with Gwen. She liked the British woman very much! She also wondered if she should try and set her father up with Gwen. They both had the medical field of a profession in common, and from the looks of her garden, they had a green thumb love as well.

Elizabeth stewed the idea over in her head. Perhaps an upcoming date night was on the horizon!

~ * ~

CHAPTER NINE ~ Date Night

A hushed silence fell over the house as Eloise made her way from the kitchen back to her bedroom.

Both Mitchell and Elizabeth had decided to go ahead and drive into town for a Sunday brunch, Eloise opting out to put her feet up and rest instead.

It wasn't unlike Eloise to retreat to her room on an odd afternoon here or there to reflect on her thoughts and feelings of the day.

Having the impromptu date invitation from Walter struck a chord deep inside, and Eloise was very much aware of how she was feeling.

She couldn't deny the fact that she found herself attracted to Walter. Something just resonated from within almost immediately, from the moment she met him. Was it Fate perhaps? After all these years alone, was there some internal clock that had resumed its ticking, telling her time was of the essence and she should consider opening herself up to dating again?

There were, simply put, too many questions and Eloise just didn't quite know what to tell herself.

Sitting on the edge of the bed, Eloise opened the nightstand drawer. Placing her leather-bound Bible back in its place, the somber woman reached for a small, tri-fold metal frame.

Opening the vintage photo frame, she gazed intently at the images. Eloise lightly ran her finger over the glass as she stared at the faces hauntingly staring back at her.

The center photograph was always the one that garnered her attention first. The image of a young woman, no more than nineteen or twenty, wearing a long white summer dress, flanked on her left by a handsome young man of equal age, donning his Sunday best. The woman held in her arms a tiny infant adorned in a little patterned yellow dress, her eyes closed.

Eloise wiped the tears from her eyes with a tissue as her gaze moved to the adjoining photos. A larger portrait photograph of the young man, smiling as he held the still sleeping baby in his arms. In the other photograph, a close-up portrait of the precious baby.

Eloise blankly looked out the bedroom window as though it wasn't the sunshine and lightly swaying palm trees she saw, but something else. Something or someone from a long time ago standing there talking to her.

"I'm sorry Mrs. Johnson," the voice of the phantom visitor could be heard resonating in her mind, "we did everything we could. I'm sorry for your loss."

Eloise was just shy of her twentieth birthday when she lay incapacitated in a hospital bed that fateful afternoon. It had been a mere two weeks from the time the photographs of her beloved husband and baby girl were taken as they celebrated their daughter's one-year birthday milestone.

The weather raged on that awful day. Her husband attempted to navigate the road from their morning service at church to her grandmother's small home on the outskirts of Savannah. The wind and rain, bellowing down with raging force, seemed hell-bent on destructing anything in its path.

It took Eloise years to finally have the courage to forgive herself for carrying the burden of guilt she could never shake. Had she not been so impatient to get to her grandmother's that day, perhaps her family would still be alive.

"Baby, we'll be there in five minutes, just keep driving!" Eloise's words were engraved in her memory. Her childhood sweetheart reluctantly continued as she turned her attention to their infant daughter who had begun crying from the backseat.

"She's hungry Marcus, let's just hurry up and get there. Besides, you drive a truck for a living. I am sure you have navigated these storms before!"

"Elle, honey, I think we should pull..."

Her husband never had a chance to finish his sentence.

Neither of them saw the tractor-trailer as it careened through the flashing traffic light, slamming their small vehicle on the driver's side. Crushing the car in seconds, the thunderous bang of the crunching metal and the cracking of the windshield like lightning streaking across the sky was all Eloise could remember until she awoke in the hospital.

Within one lifeless and tragic moment, she was left a childless widow at the tender age of nineteen.

Eloise slowly folded the aging photo frame back to its original form as she slipped it into the drawer next to her book. Closing the nightstand, she sat for a few moments, methodically rubbing her hands across both her legs as she forced herself to take several deep breaths.

"Eloise, baby, *you have got* to wake yourself up from this misery you have resigned yourself to, and start livin' your life again!" The haunting voice resonated in her mind as she visually projected the image of her grandmother reaching down as she had once done, gripping Eloise by the shoulders as though she was forcing the woman to come out of a trance.

The matriarch tried in vain to console and comfort her granddaughter through those long and heartbreaking months.

Eating very little, not wanting to leave her bed, Eloise had become intent on letting life just slip away. Death was often at the forefront of her mind, waging a daily battle with her consciousness. Her faith and her grandmother's determination were ultimately the only saving grace that kept her from taking her own life during her darkest hours.

"Leave me be, Nana."

"I'll leave you be when you start taking care of yourself again, child."

"I don't want to be here anymore, don't you understand!" Eloise had remembered telling her grandmother through a sea of tears.

"It ain't your time Eloise, it ain't your time!" Her grandmother had defiantly told her. "He has other plans for you child, he always did. His love kept you alive! I can't comfort you with a reason why they had to go, and I know you will never find closure. I won't lie to you baby girl, this is a pain you are gonna feel the rest of your days. Deep down in my heart though, I know the good Lord has a plan for you, just know that he does!"

And slowly, day by day, Eloise allowed herself to reach out to her church for guidance and support. By the end of that year, Eloise had gained employment as a caregiver for an elderly woman, and her life took a turn for the positive.

Eloise stood up from the bed as she walked over to the rental house window, gazing out over the back lawn and pool. Coming back to reality, she continued to breathe slowly as she watched various birds fly about in the bushes and trees.

She had much to be grateful for, as she reflected on her current state of affairs. After several years working as a companion and caregiver, Eloise was afforded the opportunity to move to Wilmington after her kindly employer had bequeathed her an endowment. Having lost her beloved grandmother earlier that year, and not especially close with the small family she had left, just a few cousins here and there, she decided it was time for a fresh start.

It was the early nineties when Eloise left Savannah for Wilmington, North Carolina. She found employment at a local nursing home as a caregiver while she earned her credentials as a certified nursing assistant.

As fate would have it, her calling came in the form of a roommate's knowledge of a dentist who worked as an adjunct professor in the dental hygienist program at her community college. He was desperately in need of someone to live full time in his home to help care for his terminally ill wife.

Twenty-five years later, here she was, overlooking a beautiful horizon filled with tropical plants, sunny skies, and crystal blue waters.

Just then, a little whine could be heard coming from behind Eloise's ankles. Tito raised his front paw as though to gesture he wanted something.

Eloise reached down as she gently lifted the tiny dog up and headed down the hallway towards the patio doors.

"Yes, yes, time for your potty break little man, I know!"

Eloise gave him a quick rub behind the ears as she let him out for his bathroom break.

"Scratch when you're ready to come in!" She hollered out as she gave him his instructions when he was done meandering through the yard. Within moments, the Yorkie jogged his way across the yard back to the patio door.

Scooping him back up her arms, Eloise carried her furry companion back down the hallway. Migrating towards her closet, she continued to engage in conversation with the dog.

"Well, I do believe you need to help me find something to wear tomorrow!"

The Yorkie barked as he sat dutifully on the floor, watching Eloise as she spent the rest of the afternoon busying herself with the contemplation of what outfit she would donning the following evening.

~ * ~

"Honey, you know you're welcome to join us!" Mitchell called out to Elizabeth as the trio arrived back from a short trip to the local beach. It was Monday afternoon, and they had decided to indulge in some time in the sun.

Getting their toes wet in the surf, the group was diligent in making sure they didn't overdo their stay out in the afternoon's intense rays.

Somehow, it never seems to fail. Despite valiant efforts to cover his skin with sunblock, Mitchell still ended up with a painful sunburn.

"I didn't know they would be serving fried tomatoes tonight at dinner!" Eloise couldn't resist making a teasing comment as she gave Mitchell a once-over under the fluorescent lighting.

"Yeah, yeah, always the comedian!" He shot back as he leaned in close to the large hallway mirror, cringing at the bright pink hue that now washed over his entire face, neck, and arms.

Elizabeth walked towards her father, inspecting what damage he may have incurred from the excessive sun rays. Pressing her lips together she tried to stifle a giggle.

"What?" He asked impatiently as his daughter raised her hands to cover her mouth.

"You look like a raccoon, Dad!"

"Gee, thanks! Guess I should be glad that I'm only chaperoning Eloise to her dinner date then!"

"Dinner date? You didn't mention that at lunch. Who are you going meet?"

"I didn't tell you?" Mitchell raised his brows as though he was sure he had mentioned it earlier.

"No, you didn't!"

"Well, Walter, our resident tiki bar owner slash part-time minister, invited us to join him for dinner." Mitchell paused as he looked at Eloise, who had made herself comfortable on a kitchen stool seat. Narrowing her eyes at him, he continued as he couldn't contain letting out a sarcastic chuckle.

"Really?" Elizabeth's eyes grew wide as she made the connection between her conversation the previous day with her yoga therapist, Gwen.

"Funny you should mention that." Elizabeth shifted her weight from one leg to another, rolling her barefoot toes back as she scratched her cheek. "I am pretty sure you're going on a double date with my yoga instructor, Gwendoline. She told me yesterday Walter had texted her to join him for dinner with some friends. I am going to wager to guess, that would be the two of you!"

Munching on a bowl of grapes, Eloise let out an impromptu laugh.

"Well, it looks like the fried tomato has a date after all!"

"Aw, geez, you're kidding, right?" Mitchell began to stress as he looked back at his image in the mirror.

Eloise got off her stool again as she wandered back into the foyer, her flip-flop shoes smacking her heels along the way.

"Mitchell Fisher, take off your hat." She instructed him as she stared intently at his head.

Having worn his favorite hat to the beach, it never entered his mind to take it off. He was still consciously aware of the fading lump on his forehead.

Mitchell removed the hat as his daughter, and Eloise busted out with laughter.

Mitchell reluctantly looked back in the mirror. Not only did he have raccoon eyes, but he also had a very distinct sunburn ending a few inches shy of his receding hairline.

"Maybe you should put that hat back on," Eloise blurted out, unable to contain her laughter as she poked fun of the poor man, "and the sunglasses!"

"Ha, ha, ha!" Mitchell covered his head with his hat and put his sunglasses back on his face.

"I'm going to go take a nap thank you very much. Leave you two goofballs out here to amuse yourselves!"

"Aw, Dad, I'm sorry!" Elizabeth reached over to give her father a bear hug as she tried to comfort his wounded ego.

"Don't worry about tonight, Gwen is super sweet, and she's not going to care about a little wonky sunburn!"

"Yes, she is! She's having dinner with a fried tomato, raccoon hybrid!" Eloise continued laughing as she popped another grape into her mouth.

Elizabeth turned and flicked Eloise in the arm as the woman headed back to the kitchen.

"Ignore her, Dad." The daughter turned to give her father another quick hug. "Thanks for the invite but I was thinking about calling Aidan to see if he could take me out on another kayak tour so that I could take more landscape photographs."

Elizabeth sounded a bit coy as she turned to head down the hall to her room.

"Okay honey, well, if you change your mind." Mitchell followed her as he was more than keen for a nap.

What was in store for him now? He pondered to himself as he closed his bedroom door. Sinking down onto the comfortable bed, he laid his head on the pillow and within moments was soundly snoring away.

~ * ~

By seven o'clock Mitchell and Eloise made their way out the door donning their best evening clothes. Mitchell was sure not to leave without his trusty hat, still trying to cover his head lump and uneven sunburn.

Elizabeth stood by the door as she and Tito saw the duo off for the evening.

"Have fun, don't do anything I wouldn't do," she kidded as they waved goodbye.

Waiting until the car tail lights disappeared, Elizabeth walked into the living room to retrieve her phone. Sinking into the comfortable sofa, she got up the courage to ring Aidan on his cell phone from the number on his business card.

"Hello, this is Aidan," came a voice over what was obviously a recording, "I'm either ziplining over waterfalls, backpacking the mountainside or out on the open seas enjoying a group kayak. Please leave me a detailed message, and I'll get back with you."

Letting out a slight sigh, she waited for the opportunity to leave a message.

"Um, hi Aidan, this is Elizabeth Fisher, you took me out the other day for the sea kayak excursion. I was just calling to

117

see if you offered any sunset kayaking. If you get this message, feel free to call me."

Elizabeth hit the end button on her cellular as she looked down at the Yorkie curled up next to her. Reaching over to stroke his soft fur, he was quick to glance up and give her hand a light lick.

"Well, looks like you and I are on our own this evening babe!"

Elizabeth uncrossed her legs as she rose from the sofa and headed towards the kitchen. Opening the refrigerator, she began inspecting what she might want to nibble on, having already devoured a few slices of leftover pizza after her beach outing.

Just then, her ears perked up. What sounded like her phone ringing could be heard echoing down the hall.

Elizabeth scrambled to retrieve the incoming call. Grabbing her phone, she recognized the number immediately.

"Hello." She bit her lower lip as she answered the phone.

"Hello, is this Elizabeth?" asked the young man on the other line. "This is Aidan, returning your call."

Elizabeth beamed as she looked over at Tito, who was now sitting on his hind legs watching her flurry of activity.

"Hi, how are you?" she asked as she tried not to sound nervous. "I'm sorry for calling on such short notice. I was just wondering if you might be available for an evening kayak run possibly?"

She continued flexing her lower lip with her teeth as she paced back and forth across the living room floor.

"Well, I wish I could say I was, however, John just took a last-minute reservation. A rather large group is having a family reunion, so, unfortunately, he's left in the truck with all of our kayaks."

The young woman, feeling disappointed scrambled to find something to say. "I completely understand, it was last minute I know, I honestly should have called much sooner."

"Hey, no worries," answered the polite voice on the other end. After a slight pause of silence, Aidan could be heard clearing his throat.

"Do you like motorcycles at all by chance?"

"Um, gosh, I haven't been on one in ages, but yeah, I use to have a friend that I would go riding with…why?"

"Well," the young man paused again briefly, "I was thinking, since I can't take you out for a water excursion, perhaps you would you be interested in a bike ride up to the pier? You could get some great shots there and then maybe we could go hit Walter's for some evening karaoke and a bite to eat?"

Elizabeth whirled around to give Tito a wide-eyed smile. "Sure, that be cool!"

"Great! Wear your trekking shoes, jeans, and a long-sleeved shirt. I can supply the helmet."

After a few more moments exchanging her address, Elizabeth hung up the phone.

Running to her room with Tito in hot pursuit, she quickly rummaged through her closet pulling out the appropriate attire, knowing that it wouldn't take long for Aidan to arrive.

"I'm not sure if it's a date or what, but at least he called!" She gave her furry companion a quick cuddle as she headed to the bathroom to freshen up, excited at the prospects of spending the evening out with the handsome Irishman!

~ * ~

"Aloha!" Walter greeted Mitchell and Eloise as they made their way into the resort's foyer. The interior, ornately decorated in native Hawaiian décor, was filled with mingling guests. Voices echoed up and down the expansive hallways as people made their way to the various function rooms on the main level of the hotel.

Walter reached out as he shook Mitchell's hand before turning his attention to Eloise.

Taking her hand gently, he gave it a light kiss as he complimented the blushing woman on her smartly dressed outfit and stunning evening appearance.

"I'm so glad you both could join us!" Walter turned his attention briefly to the pretty woman standing by his side. Eloquently dressed in a flowing two-piece pantsuit, Gwendoline extended her hand in a polite gesture of greeting.

"Eloise, Mitchell," he began as he stepped back slightly, "this is my lovely friend, Gwen!"

"It's very nice to meet you both." The woman kindly responded.

Eloise smiled as she reached out to shake Gwen's hand. Mitchell took Gwen's hand firmly in his as he nodded.

Feeling slightly embarrassed that he was still wearing his hat inside the formal setting, Mitchell suddenly felt the need to explain his situation.

"You'll have to forgive me, everyone," he grinned sheepishly as he tipped the hat slightly with his forefinger, "I had a bit of an accident the other day, and I'm afraid my forehead is still in recovery mode along with this ridiculous sunburn!"

"Oh dear, nothing serious I hope!" Gwen, being the nurse that she was, quickly spoke up.

Now, aware that everyone was staring at his head, Mitchell tried to play it off. "Oh, no, just a little bump from an incident in the backyard."

"Yes," Eloise wasted no time to jump on the bandwagon, "Mitchell and a tree decided to play a little game of Roulette...well, as you can obviously see, the branch won!"

Mitchell pursed his lips together as he looked at Eloise. Realizing she just eased the awkward moment as both Walter and Gwen began to laugh at the joke, he gave his friend a cynical smile. Eloise obliged by raising her eyebrows in her 'I told you so' manner, quick to see the joke helped lighten the mood.

"Well, thankfully no serious injuries incurred and it hasn't spoiled your trip!" Walter laughed as he pitched into the conversation with a husky voice.

The group headed towards the open-air patio of the restaurant as a maître de took them to their table.

The restaurant was a flurry of activity as large groups of people made their way to their tables, mingling with one another or just enjoying the views over the ocean as the sun began to set slowly. Bursts of orange and pink hues painted the beautiful sky in an array of colors.

Engaging in small talk while perusing the menu, they took their time to order drinks as they decided on their choice selections.

"Well, Mitchell, I hear that you are a retired dentist?" Gwen directed her question as she thanked the waiter for her drink.

"Information provided by my daughter, I would imagine." Mitchell smiled as he was now while aware of the connection between the British woman and Elizabeth.

"She did tell me, yes, and what a sweet and thoughtful thing to do, giving her father such a wonderful retirement gift!"

Both Mitchell and Eloise smiled. Even with all the crazy events that had occurred since their arrival, they were grateful for Elizabeth's thoughtful gift.

"We couldn't be more proud of our Elizabeth, she's a good kid." Mitchell nodded his head as he reflected on his daughter's generously bestowed holiday.

"I couldn't agree with you more, she is a lovely young woman," Gwen added as she reached for her drink, smiling in Mitchell's direction.

The group continued with their conversation as they enjoyed a delicious meal while listening to music from a band in the background. As their plates were cleared from the table, Walter took the initiative to ask Eloise for a dance. Flattered,

Eloise accepted as Mitchell, following Walter's lead, invited Gwen to join him on the dance floor.

The two couples joined several others already enjoying themselves as they danced to the live music.

"You will have to forgive me," Mitchell stated as he led Gwen onto the dance floor, "I don't think I've had a proper dance since I was in college with my wife."

"I'm sure you miss her dearly." Gwen gave him a warm smile as she reflected on the conversation at the dinner table. Getting to know one another, all four spoke briefly of their pasts, their spouses, and their livelihoods. Feeling very comfortable with one another, they all opened about their life experiences.

"We cannot stop the clock of life. We simply make the most of the time we have while we are here with the ones we love." She added as they migrated their way across the floor doing a traditional nightclub two-step dance.

Gwen complimented Mitchell on his dance abilities, finding that surprisingly, he was rather good.

"I suppose I haven't lost my technique for the basic steps after all!" He laughed, surprising himself by remembering the moves. He admitted early in his marriage before Elizabeth was born, he and his wife had taken ballroom dancing classes together.

"Well, see, you are quite the professional already!" Gwen winked as she admired his skills.

"I wouldn't say that, but I am certainly relieved not to be dancing with two left feet this evening."

Glancing over at Eloise, Mitchell gave his friend a wide grin as showed off his dance skills.

Eloise continued to blush as she slow danced with Walter. She felt truly smitten with the man as she could sense his generous and kindly nature during their dinner conversation.

While everyone else had intimately spoken about their families, Eloise opted not to divulge too many details about her past, focusing instead on telling them about her charity work with her church and her hobbies. The last thing she wanted for the evening she was enjoying so much, was to feel pity from their new acquaintances.

As the dinner and dancing had drawn to a close, the foursome made their way to the parking lot. Having enjoyed their evening, they all agreed to get together again soon as they bid each other a good night.

~ * ~

Elizabeth could hear the squeal of tires on the pavement as she peered out of the foyer's window to see Aidan pulling into the driveway. Kissing Tito on the head, she gave the Yorkie one of his favorite snacks as she watched him trot down the hallway to her room.

Satisfied she had what she wanted to bring with her, Elizabeth made her way out to greet him.

Perched atop the motorcycle, Aidan smiled as he dismounted the cruiser.

Reaching for the spare helmet he had secured to the passenger seat, he grinned and watched her reaction as she admired the bike.

"Wow, what a gorgeous ride!"

"Thank you!" Aidan replied proudly to her compliment, "I had a custom paint job done this year. In honor of the ocean and the sky, I found the perfect shade of blue, and I couldn't be more pleased with it."

Elizabeth tightened her backpack straps to secure in place the bag on her back. Making sure her modular helmet was on properly, she tucked wisps of loose hair back from her eyes. She quickly adjusted her sunglasses, then gave Aidan a 'thumbs up' as he slowly maneuvered the motorcycle out of the driveway.

Giving Elizabeth's leg a light pat, was his signal he was ready to speed off. Instinctively grabbing his waist, she giggled to herself as they sped down the residential lane and onto the highway.

Closing her eyes, the young woman allowed herself the freedom to take in and absorb the fresh air massaging her face. As Aidan increased the speed of the bike, they both lowered their protective visors to guard against the unwanted advances of an odd bug or any other debris in the air.

It was still early in the evening as the couple enjoyed a long ride down the highway and up a few remote coastal roads. After an hour of cruising, Aidan made his way back in the direction of the Kapalei Bay. Just as the sun began to set in the sky, adorning it with a burst of citrus colors, the pair made their way down a long wooden pier. The light wind cast the potent smell of salt water into the air.

Raising her sunglasses over her head, Elizabeth set to work getting her camera and lens set up on her compact, portable tripod.

Spending several minutes engaging in conversation, the two laughed at Aidan's jokes as he watched with admiration while Elizabeth explained various industry terminology as she guided him through the process of setting up for the 'perfect' shot.

"Honestly, I can take a hundred shots of the same thing and only see two or three I like the best."

"I think I'm going to have to hire you to do some updated photographs for my website!" He grinned as he viewed the images on her LCD screen.

"Well, I am available for hire, here's my card!" She added, giving him a wink as she pulled one of her business cards out of a pocket in the camera bag.

As the sun began to sink into the horizon, the duo stayed a few more minutes as they watched light waves lap against the pier while enjoying the array of activity surrounding them. Families enjoying a late afternoon of fishing began to pack up their things as a few other couples stood along the pier, also admiring the view.

"Well, why don't we go get something to eat and enjoy witnessing a few karaoke victims belting their hearts out." Aidan quipped as he reached for their helmets.

"As long as you don't drag me up there I'm perfectly fine with that!" Elizabeth pleaded as they headed towards the parking lot.

"I can't make any promises."

"Oh, my gosh, please don't make me get up there, I will die of embarrassment! The only one who can sing in my family is Eloise, and she can put anyone to shame!"

"Alright then, I expect a standing ovation showing your full support to the expert here." Aidan jokingly gestured at himself as she nodded in agreement.

"Done!"

Without thinking twice, Aidan put his arm over Elizabeth's shoulder as he guided them both to his bike.

As the evening wore on, Elizabeth thoroughly enjoyed every minute of it. Aidan, being quite the musician, serenaded a small gathering at the tiki bar with his renditions of various songs, all the while strumming away on one of the guitars Walter stored in the corner of the stage. After a couple of hours of entertaining themselves, the couple made their way back to Elizabeth's home.

Walking her up to the door, Aidan thanked Elizabeth for the enjoyable evening out.

She thanked him in return for the fun night and while she had it fresh in her mind, set up a date for Aidan to take her family out for a waterfall excursion.

Putting his hands in his pockets, Aidan propped himself up against the stone façade of the front porch.

"It's nice to have an evening out with someone besides John, no offense to him of course!" Aidan laughed as he referred to his business partner.

"Well, I'm more than happy to be out with someone other than just my dad and Eloise for a change, not that I don't love them both to pieces!"

"From the sounds of it, you just might be seeing less of them and more of me then, should they hit it off with Walter and Gwen." Aidan winked at Elizabeth as she blushed slightly.

I certainly don't have any problem with that proposition! She smiled at the thought of spending more time with Aidan.

Deciding what to do next, Elizabeth stepped up on her tippy toes and kissed Aidan on the cheek.

Looking slightly surprised, the young man leaned over and reciprocated by hugging her.

Respecting the grounds of the young man wanting to maintain his professionalism, since Elizabeth was a client, she was content with his subtle yet thoughtful gesture. Bidding him a good night, she unlocked the front door and waved as he made his way out of the driveway, watching as the motorcycle disappeared into the darkness.

Dropping the house key into the bowl in the foyer, Elizabeth absently made her way down the long hallway towards her bedroom.

Greeted by a sleepy Tito, the young woman scooped her dog up as she playfully rubbed his ears.

"Looks like your mom here may have more outings soon with a certain, handsome Irishman!"

Letting out a little yap, the cute Yorkie wagged his tail as she let him out in the backyard to do his business. Still daydreaming about her next outing with Aidan, she was looking forward to gossiping with Eloise about their dates!

~ * ~

"Well, I think that was a very nice evening, wouldn't you agree?" Mitchell turned his attention briefly to Eloise who was busy touching up her lipstick in the visor mirror.

"I will be honest with you Fisher, it's been a long time since I met someone I could connect with…well, you know what I mean." Eloise struggled to find the right words as she attempted to explain what it was she was feeling.

"Fisher, we're like brother and sister. It never mattered that we came from two diverse backgrounds, we were still the same ya know." Eloise's perfectly manicured brows furrowed as she spoke. "We're good people with big hearts!"

Eloise raised her hand to her face as she lightly touched her cheek, deep in thought. "We had a common bond, Joanna, and we both knew the pains of losing the ones we loved so dearly."

With his free hand, Mitchell gave Eloise a light pat on her outstretched arm. "You're my family Elle, you and Elizabeth. There will never be enough words that I could convey to express my gratitude for having you in my life."

Mitchell gave his companion a warm smile as they turned onto the highway to head for home.

"You're my best friend, Eloise Johnson."

Eloise beamed as she reached out and patted Mitchell on the shoulder.

"I love you too, Mitchell Carmichael Fisher!" She winked as she flicked him in the ear with her finger.

A few moments later, Mitchell let out a chuckle as he gave Eloise a side glance.

"Since when are you into tickling my neck?"

Looking confused, Eloise leaned slightly to the right as she laughed, "What are you on about Fisher? I'm not tickling you!"

Mitchell took the steering wheel with his right hand as he reached his now freed left hand up behind his head.

"Well, if that's not your nails digging into my neck, whose are they?" He attempted to make a joke as he thought for sure it was Eloise's hand and arm he felt pressing down on his traps muscle.

Then, in the broken silence they both heard a low and throaty gurgling sound.

Eloise shot her arm back as her eyes grew wide, pushing herself back against her door frozen in fear. "What the heck!"

Two distinct sets of claws were gripping the man's neck as the reptile clambered its way onto his hat.

"Get it off me!" Mitchell hollered as the girth of the lizard weighed heavily on his hat, causing the poor man temporary blindness from the road.

"I'm not touching it! Oh, my sweet Jesus, it's *on your head!*"

"I know that Elle, for crying out loud, I can't see the damn road!"

Eloise scrambled to grab the steering wheel as the angry lizard hissed at Mitchell's clumsy attempts to secure a hold of the creature. Failing in his ability to get his hands firmly around the lizard, Mitchell did the only thing he could think to do. He smacked the ginormous gecko across its face in hopes it would jump off his head.

He realized just at that moment, attempting to hit the confused creature wasn't the smartest decision he could have made.

Like an old film winding down in slow motion, the inevitable was about to happen. The angry lizard went airborne as it flipped itself off Mitchell's hat. Performing the aerial maneuver, it twisted its body around as it landed on Mitchell's chest. Then without warning, like a suction cup, clamping onto Mitchell's face.

"*Oh, my God...I'm living in a horror movie!*" Eloise cried out as she closed her eyes for a moment. Still holding the steering wheel as the car veered out of control across the road, all the while trying to lean her head as far away from Mitchell and the angry gecko.

"He must have climbed into the car back at the house when the top was down!" Eloise hollered out as an afterthought.

"AHHHH!" Mitchell cried out as the reptile bit firmly down on his nose. "AHHHH fuu..." and before he could even finish his sentence, his anguish was stifled as he heard his companion scream out in terror.

Jolted from the searing pain, Mitchell inadvertently sped the car up as he jerked his head back while frantically attempting to grab the lizard with both hands.

Squirming out of Mitchell's grasp, the squawking lizard made a flying leap in Eloise's direction, landing squarely on the hysterical woman's bosom.

131

"There is a two-foot lizard on my boobs, oh Lord Jesus, *get it off me!*" The distraught woman screamed, her arms waving wildly in the air. Ignoring his pain, Mitchell tried frantically to reach over and grab the reptile off Eloise's chest.

"Put your arms down Elle. I can't reach it!"

"You are grabbing in all the wrong places!" She continued hollering as the lizard scrambled back and forth across her now heavily panting chest.

"It's stuck! Oh, my goodness, its claws are caught in my bra, Mitchell!" Eloise couldn't calm herself down as she began to hyperventilate. The lizard barked loudly as it tugged at its claw hooked to the strap of her undergarment.

Panic-stricken, Mitchell tried to keep his eye on the road as he steered with his left hand while trying to grab the lizard with his free hand. Too fazed to think to hit the brakes, his eyes were tearing up from the pain of the facial bite coupled with his companion's hysteria.

"Pull over, Mitchell!" Eloise continued her screaming as the lizard managed to free its stuck claw.

Without thinking Mitchell slammed on the breaks. At that same moment, the confused and equally frightened reptile leaped from Eloise's blouse to the headrest then onto the back seat of the car.

Only it came a few seconds too late as their convertible ricocheted off the backside of an idling vehicle stopped at a stop light.

In shock, they both looked at each other, too stunned to move.

"Did that just happen?" Mitchell spoke in disbelief.

Eloise couldn't contain herself. Through the craziness of it all, and the sheer frustration, she began to laugh.

Mitchell couldn't help but start laughing himself.

"Your face is beginning to look like a war zone, Fisher!"

"I think your chest just saw more action than it has in thirty years!"

Both couldn't hold back the tears of laughter, still shaking their heads in disbelief.

"On top of it all, I think I just rear-ended a cop."

"Oh, goodness gracious, I don't even know what to think." Eloise leaned forward as she propped her forehead in the palms of her hands.

Just then a light tap could be heard on the driver's side window.

Lowering the window, Mitchell, now holding a handkerchief to his face peered out into the darkness.

"Mr. Fisher, step out of the vehicle."

"I can explain, Officer Kahele."

"Step out of the vehicle, Mr. Fisher." The firm and familiar voice repeated its command.

Mitchell unlocked his seatbelt as he slowly made his way out of the car.

Officer Kahele stood erect as he crossed his arms firmly over his chest.

"Have you been drinking tonight, Mr. Fisher?"

"No, well, I mean, well yes." Mitchell scrambled to answer the question. "If you will let me explain."

"How many drinks have you had this evening Mr. Fisher?"

"Only one, honestly, and that was a few hours ago. Just hear me out." Mitchell motioned to the car as he attempted to explain to the dubious officer what had happened.

"So, basically you're telling me some lizard performing acrobatic aerial maneuvers just flew out of nowhere and landed on your face?"

"I know, I know, it sounds crazy!"

"I just worked a sixteen-hour shift between two jobs. I'm on my way home to some peace and quiet when you come out of nowhere, ramming into the back of my vehicle." Officer Kahele continued to stare Mitchell squarely in the eyes as he shifted his hands to his hips. "You honestly expect me to believe some cockamamie story about a giant gecko jumping on your head?"

"No, really, I'm not kidding." Mitchell turned to look towards the backseat of the now slightly-dented convertible. "It's still sitting in the backseat. I mean, just look at my face."

Calling out from inside the car, Eloise confirmed Mitchell's story.

"It's still sitting here, Officer Kahele!" Eyes wide, Eloise pointed to the backseat. "Shoot, the poor man has teeth marks all over that big ole nose of his!"

Pressing his lips together, the annoyed officer took a step forward as he shined his flashlight on Mitchell's face.

Blinded by the light, Mitchell took a step backward as he raised his hand to shield his eyes.

Noticing what did look like an obvious bit mark from the jaws of some creature on Mitchell's face, Officer Kahele approached the vehicle. Leaning his large, upper torso into the back of the car it took him only a moment to make a confirmation that the wild-eyed couple, were in fact, telling the truth.

Letting out a huge sigh, the perplexed officer pulled a small notepad from his holster. Glancing at Mitchell, who was still standing motionless cupping the white cloth to his bloodied face, the policeman began writing in his booklet.

"Mr. Fisher, unfortunately, I am still going to write you a citation. Lizard or no lizard, you are at fault for causing a rear-end collision."

Mitchell, hugely relieved that the officer wasn't going to drag him to jail, stood quietly as the uniformed civil servant finished writing out the ticket.

"If you would like to avoid having negative points posted to your driving record, I would recommend that you take our weekend driver improvement course, Mr. Fisher." Officer Kahele gave Mitchell a quick once-over glance as he smugly continued. "No doubt, at your age, your insurance company would be rather keen to jack your rates up."

Trying not to respond and say something he might regret, Mitchell dutifully took the ticket.

"Um, do I need to drive with that thing in my backseat?"

Rolling his eyes, the police officer motioned Mitchell to move as he leaned into the vehicle and carefully removed the docile reptile from the backseat.

"Open your trunk, Mr. Fisher."

The officer carefully placed the lizard in the trunk as he turned to look at Mitchell. "He belongs in his natural habitat. When you get home, pop your trunk so he can let himself out."

He continued to give the wide-eyed man sharp stare. "Don't forget to let him out of the trunk!"

Officer Kahele walked back to the driver's side of the car and instructed Mitchell to close his eyes. Shining the flashlight again on the poor man's face, the officer checked the flesh wound.

"Looks like a superficial wound, you won't need stitches." The brooding man hovered over Mitchell as he inspected the facial injury. "Clean it thoroughly when you get home. If you have any suspicious swelling, there's a small after-hours medical facility down by the supermarket. They can prescribe a round of antibiotics if needed."

Nodding his head feverishly, Mitchell climbed into his car.

Leaning into the driver's side window and staring firmly at Mitchell, the officer rubbed his cleanly shaved chin as he seemed to ponder a deep thought.

"You have got to be the most problematic person I have ever met Fisher...or just the unluckiest individual I have ever met."

Shaking his head, the tired officer headed back to his vehicle.

"Ain't that the truth!" Eloise couldn't resist answering the officer's statement once he was well out of earshot.

Riding in silence, the pair finally arrived home.

"Pop the trunk Mitchell!"

"Yep, got it!"

"You're going to have to call the car rental in the morning."

"How do I explain this one?" Mitchell chuckled softly.

"Hello, there folks, I had a minor fender bender in your car. I was attacked last night by a psycho, ninja flipping lizard." Eloise pretended to talk in a dramatic sounding voice.

Both laughed as they made their way to the front door. Thoroughly exhausted, they quietly entered the house so as not to wake Elizabeth.

"She just might ban us both from driving. It's just a few scratches, and no one would ever notice. We keep this to ourselves?" Mitchell asked.

"Agreed!"

~ * ~

CHAPTER TEN ~ The Wishing Well

"Come on, Elle, it will be fun!" Elizabeth continued her attempts to coax Eloise into going with them on Aidan's guided tour.

Several days had passed since their evenings out with Walter, Gwen, and Aidan. The three of them felt like they were beginning to settle into the island life.

Elizabeth continued to enjoy her morning group yoga classes at Gwen's retreat as well as her private sessions with the practitioner.

Mitchell had decided to exchange gardening for a few rounds at the local golf course, sans tokay geckos! Eloise, for her part, enjoyed having time to herself at the house to indulge in her ritual morning talk shows, and afternoons spent lounging in the hammock reading a book or taking a dip in the pool. She also discreetly found the opportunity to see Walter by joining an evening service at the church, admittedly the highlight of her week.

"Exactly how much hiking is involved?"

"I don't know, some."

"So, let me get this right. You want me to hike all the way up a mountain to watch a bunch of water pour over the side of it. *Then*, hike all the way back down again, is that right?" Not exactly a fan of outdoor adventures, Eloise narrowed her eyes at the prospect of the strenuous activity.

"It's just a little bit of walking, Elle!" Mitchell rolled his eyes as he attempted to help his daughter in her struggle to convince the skeptical woman to go with them, "It's not going to kill you to get out your shoes and go with us."

"Exactly!" Elizabeth answered as her father raised his brows, giving Eloise a slight glare.

Deciding to try a different tactic she use to take as a child, Elizabeth migrated from her breakfast chair onto Eloise's lap. Wrapping her arms around the woman's shoulders, she stared directly into her eyes. "I want you to come with us, and I won't take 'no' for an answer!"

Planting a kiss on Eloise's cheek after she reluctantly agreed to go, Elizabeth headed down the hallway towards her room, calling out over her shoulder, "Aidan will be here in an hour to pick us up!"

Eloise turned her attention to Mitchell as she rolled her eyes to the ceiling.

"Lord help me, the things I do for that child!"

"Oh, come on, it will give you some exciting to do."

"Since when, in all the years you have known me Fisher, have I ever gotten the glee of excitement in taking a hiking trip?"

"Well, you remember there was the time we did manage to talk you into a weekend camping trip when she was in junior high school."

"Yeah, then it poured rained *all* night long, and I finally made you pack everything up and check us into a hotel!" Eloise cocked her head to the side as she narrowed her eyes at him.

"You felt so guilty that was I forced to sleep half the night on a deflated air mattress in a dingy tent during monsoon season. Oh, and the humidity…do not get me started on the humidity. You knew better than ever to ask me to do that again!"

"Okay, yeah, well…there was *that time!*"

Eloise, making her point, eased herself out of her chair. Reaching for her coffee cup, she patted Mitchell on the back as she turned to leave the breakfast room.

"Seeing as how I have to exert my energies this afternoon, I thank you in advance for offering to clear the breakfast table."

Mitchell laughed as he watched Eloise saunter down the hallway towards her room, still pouting over having to take part in the afternoon excursion.

"You'll have fun, Elle, trust me!"

Not missing a beat, she paused for a moment as she turned to shake her finger at him.

"Fun for me is shopping with your credit card Mitchell Fisher, and you know better than to end a sentence in my general direction with a 'trust me' attached to it!"

Mitchell rolled his eyes as he chuckled slightly. Well, she did have a point with that one!

~ * ~

A light drizzle had begun as the group made their way into the Kapahani Falls State Park two hours later. Not wanting to miss the opportunity to spend more time with Aidan, Elizabeth convinced Eloise to join them and not sit in the parked truck all afternoon.

"It's just a little rain, and you are not going to melt!"

"Child, I'm only doing this for you!"

140

"I checked the weather report for this afternoon, and we weren't expecting any rain. I'm a bit surprised," Mitchell stated in a slightly perplexed voice as he squinted his eyes while glancing up at the overcast sky.

"I completely understand if you guys don't want to venture up there." Aidan looked solemnly at the trio. "I do, however, keep a dozen or so travel ponchos in the back of the truck. He pointed to the direction of the rear of his vehicle as he made his way towards the utility box to unlock it.

Not giving her father or Eloise a chance to change their minds, Elizabeth was quick to interject.

"We'll be fine Aidan. A little drizzle won't hurt us!"

"Well, we will have to be cautious once we hike up there. If it starts raining any heavier, we will have to be on the lookout for mudslides."

Elizabeth turned her attention quickly to Eloise. Standing with her hands on her hips, Eloise narrowed her eyes and looked as though she was about to say something.

"Please!" Elizabeth motioned silently with her lips as she held her hands up in front of her chest, making a plea motion.

Eloise pursed her lips together as she reluctantly took one of the see-through ponchos from Aidan. Standing there for a moment while the others gathered their backpacks, she placed her hands on her hips again, looking up momentarily to the sky.

"I do not have a good feeling about this!" she whispered to herself as she let out a huge sigh.

~ * ~

Twenty minutes had passed since the group departed from the car park, making their way into the rainforest. Following a designated path laid out for hikers, they continued to forge ahead to their destination.

Dense vegetation shadowed the narrow, man-made walk path as a loud gushing sound could be heard in the near vicinity.

"The Kapahani Falls are just ahead," Aidan called out to the group as he stopped briefly to check on everyone following his lead.

Giving Elizabeth a wide grin, he placed his hand on her shoulder as she stepped up her pace to move ahead of him. Blushing for a moment, she returned a smile as she readjusted her backpack under the waterproof poncho.

"Almost there, folks!" Aidan waited patiently as Mitchell made his way up the path, followed by a less-than-thrilled Eloise, drudging her way past the young man.

Coming to a clearing in the woods, the group stopped next to the safety fence as they admired the massive waterfall. Due to the rains, a significant amount of water had accumulated in the river. Pouring over a hundred-foot drop, they watched as mist rose from the pool below.

"Oh my gosh, look you guys!" Elizabeth pointed in the direction of the water basin as she began to unload her camera gear from her backpack.

As the sun attempted to shine through the thicket of clouds, a rainbow had begun to form over the waterfall, cascading down into the water basin that now filled a long-extinct volcanic crater.

"Honey, that should make for some pretty photographs," Mitchell commented to his daughter as he admired the imagery of the colored spectrum giving way to the lush green forest and mist covered waters.

Elizabeth gave her father a quick grin as she moved around the observation area, snapping up dozens of photographs.

"You have to admit, Elle, it sure is pretty." Mitchell coaxed his companion as he gave her a slight nudge.

Rolling her eyes, she reluctantly agreed that it was quite a vision to behold!

Aidan gave a history lesson of the area as Elizabeth took photographs of everyone, utilizing the scenic imagery as a backdrop.

Mitchell couldn't help but find himself amused by the rush of water flowing from the waterfall into the vast river basin below. Reaching into his front pocket, he pulled out a penny. Chuckling aloud, he turned his attention to the trio standing beside him.

"Do you think it will grant me a wish then?" he called out as he held the penny in the air.

"Um, sir, I probably wouldn't do that if I were you." Aidan stepped back slightly from the guardrail as he watched Mitchell leaning forward, hand already in motion as he tossed the penny with full force into the air in the direction of the waterfall.

Still oblivious to his actions, Mitchell stood proudly with his hands on his hips as he turned his attention back to the others.

"Bet you can't guess what I wished for!"

"A reprieve from a ticket for littering perhaps?" Eloise was sharp to snap back.

"Why would you say that?" Mitchell looked perplexed as he thought his little antic was harmless.

"Well, Mr. Fisher, volcanos are sacred to the natives of the islands." Aidan pursed his lips together as he lightly scratched his forehead. Not wanting to offend his client but feeling the need to inform him of his actions he continued. "Kapahani Falls is a known sacred burial site. It would be like littering in a religious temple, you just kind of shouldn't do it."

The rest of the group stood quietly as they watched Mitchell squirm under the awkward silence. No sooner did Aidan give his lecture, a large groaning could be heard radiating from the sky. Within moments the sky darkened, the small sliver of sunlight that had cast its last ray down on the waterfall was now gone. A heavy rain began to fall on the group.

"Time to head back guys, we don't want to get stuck out here with potential mudslides." Aidan quickly gathered the trio as he motioned them towards the trail.

Just then, a loud and startling 'BOOM' deafened the air from the sky. Loud claps of thunder could be heard as they quickly began to make their descent down the narrow rainforest path.

"Dad, what were you thinking?" Elizabeth hollered over the thunderous noises emanating from the now blackened sky. They struggled to keep their balance as they made their way down the uneven footpath, frantically trying not to slip and fall.

The group hurriedly made their way down the trail as murky, mud-filled water began rushing its way down the hillside.

"Mitchell Fisher, what in the hell were you thinking?" Eloise panted heavily as she attempted to keep her balance. "It's a sacred waterfall, not a damn wishing well!"

"Well, I didn't exactly think the sky would open up and drop the motherload on us!"

"Guys, I'm sure it's just a coincidence…I think!" Elizabeth attempted to explain as they continued to hurry their way back down the drenched pathway.

"Please be careful of your footing!" Aidan hollered out as he took up the rear of the group. Ensuring he had a visual of everyone as they reached out towards various tree limbs to grab for balance.

"Gee Mitchell, what was that you said about how a little hike wouldn't kill anyone?" Eloise yelled over her shoulder as she clung to a large branch for balance.

Elizabeth stopped to catch her breath as the group finally made their way to a clearing where they no longer felt they were in danger.

Bending over slightly, clutching her side, she attempted to breathe into the pain she was suddenly feeling. Not wanting to generate too much attention, she forced herself to stand upright.

Mitchell was quick to observe his daughter's actions. "Honey, are you okay?"

"Yeah, Dad, I'm fine." Elizabeth clenched her teeth as she tried to force a smile. Not sure if she was feeling beads of sweat or the raindrops running down her face, she quickly used her hand to wipe the moisture from her forehead and cheeks.

Tucking a few stray hairs back into her headscarf, she blinked her eyes several times. She was consciously aware that the pain she was feeling seemed far more aggressive than the few previous episodes she had begun to experience since they arrived on the island.

"Just running pains I'm sure!"

"Here, hop on." Aidan quickly advanced towards Elizabeth as he lowered himself down in front of her. Swinging his backpack to the front of his chest, he motioned for her to climb onto his back.

Feeling some relief, she obediently followed his direction as she clambered onto his back.

Physically fit and use to carrying camping gear on strenuous walks, Aidan straightened his posture as he walked with ease while Elizabeth lightly bounced in unison to his strides.

Smiling at Eloise, she sheepishly waved as she was keenly aware of the woman's discontent for the afternoon's adventure.

Not moving from her spot, Eloise slowly turned around to look Mitchell squarely in the eyes, giving him her signature, 'you know I want something' grin.

"Don't even think about it." Mitchell wasted no time reading into her motives.

"I'm tired, I'm wet, and my feet hurt!"

"I'm the one with a bad back. I think you should give me the piggyback ride." He was quick to retort.

"You would say that now wouldn't you, Fisher!"

"Would another shopping trip tomorrow make you feel better?" Mitchell tried to smooth the situation over with his companion. Knowing full well the 'incident' on the mountain had been a reminder of their failed camping trip all those years before.

Rolling her eyes mockingly as though she was deep in thought, she wasted no time answering him.

"That just might suffice."

Reaching her hand again to her head, she clutched a chunk of hair in her fist.

Putting extra emphasis on her words, Eloise narrowed her eyes as she continued to stare at Mitchell. "You do realize this monsoon rain and humidity have put quite a damper, *literally*, on my beloved locks!"

Mitchell hoisted his travel satchel up onto his shoulder as he shuffled past Eloise, aware of her intimidation tactics.

"Shopping coupled with a trip to the spa, how's that?"

Eloise quickly picked up her pace as she brushed past Mitchell, adding a little extra emphasis to her walk.

"Gee, I think my feet are feeling better already!"

~ * ~

After a nearly disastrous afternoon, Aidan returned everyone safely to the house. Anxious to get out of their damp clothing, Mitchell and Eloise all but knocked each other over racing for the front door.

Bidding Aidan a goodbye, Elizabeth thanked him for trying to make the best of the day. They had already made plans to do an overnight camping hike through Na Pali in two days, and she was keen to see him again.

Agreeing they were all thoroughly exhausted and in need of cleaning up, everyone dispersed to their respective rooms for showers and rest. Deciding on ordering in for dinner so they could relax the remainder of the day, they all agreed the day had brought more than any of them had expected!

Elizabeth sat quietly in her bathroom as she listened for the sound of running water coming from her father and Eloise's rooms.

Giving Tito a scratch behind the ears as the little dog lay curled up at her feet, Elizabeth pulled out the business card given to her by Gwen the week before from her wallet.

Dialing the number on the card, she waited patiently as she heard the voice on the other end of the line retrieve the call.

"Good afternoon, Kapalei Clinic, may I help you?" The sound of a friendly voice could be heard on the receiving end of the phone call.

"Um, yes, my name is Elizabeth Fisher. I was given a referral for your clinic. I've been experiencing some frequent pains in my lower sides and back, and I was hoping I could get an appointment to see Dr. Estrada if he's available this week?"

Elizabeth waited patiently as the receptionist on the phone checked the clinic's schedule. Biting nervously at her lip, she tried to force any negative and fearful thoughts out of her mind. Feeling her anxiety trying to get the better of her, she closed her eyes as she took several deep breaths.

"Well, we do have an appointment available tomorrow afternoon at two o'clock. A cancellation that was called in this morning." The voice responded as Elizabeth perked up hearing how quickly she could be seen.

"I'll take that, thank you!" Elizabeth hung up the phone as she confirmed the appointment.

Setting her phone on the vanity counter, Elizabeth started a bath for herself. Putting her focus on the warm water filling the bathtub, the nervous woman tried to shake the feeling of anxiety creeping up inside of her.

It's nothing silly girl! She tried to tell herself.

Remembering back to all the times she would feel thoroughly exhausted after a long day in the field doing a photo shoot, she continued to remind herself it was probably nothing more than fatigue or perhaps her medication being bothersome.

In any event, Elizabeth felt it best to make the appointment as a safeguard against anything more serious. She had been so diligent in the last few years looking after her health.

Elizabeth closed her eyes again as she leaned back against the padded bath pillow. Trying to keep positive thoughts in her mind, she smiled as she contemplated the overnight camping excursion she planned with Aidan for that week.

Reaching over the bathtub ledge, she tickled Tito on the nose. "Let's just keep this appointment between us for now," she whispered, "shall we little man? No need in getting Dad or Eloise all bent out of shape over what is most likely nothing!"

~ * ~

CHAPTER ELEVEN ~ An Overnight Excursion

Dr. Estrada watched with concern as Elizabeth rubbed her hands together anxiously. Looking up to make eye contact with him, she bit her lower lip as she slowly began to relay the details of her previous medical history.

"It's been six months since I had my last checkup. Everything in my bloodwork came back normal. Honestly, I have felt pretty good up until maybe a few weeks ago."

Elizabeth tried to stop fidgeting in her chair as she continued for several minutes to give the physician an accurate account of her health history.

"That's why I want to go ahead and run the bloodwork, the best option we have right now is to try and rule out what could or could not be an underlying cause. The nurse will be in shortly with release forms so that I can obtain your records from your doctors in New York."

Elizabeth listened intently to the doctor as she nervously began to shake one of her legs, an anxious habit she had developed as a teen. Conscious of her behavior, she forced herself to stop.

Noticing his patient's anxiety, the doctor quickly leaned forward, reaching out to pat her on the hand.

"You've been through a lot in the last few years Elizabeth. I understand that the element of the unknown can be frightening. That's why I want to be sure what we are dealing with here."

"I know, I should have been seen for a follow-up much sooner than now. I guess, part of me just doesn't want to think something is wrong." Elizabeth shook her head as she blamed herself for not seeing her doctor sooner.

"Knowing now that you have been showing signs of these symptoms for a few months, it's essential that we try and put your mind at ease, as well as your body by finding out what the underlying condition could be."

Elizabeth nodded her head as she listened intently.

A gentle knock could be heard at the door, as the nurse entered with a small packet of paperwork.

"Jennifer will explain the release statements to you. We will get those out today so that we can have your records sent to us."

After a few moments with the nurse, signing all the forms, the doctor returned to the clinic room as the young woman gathered her belongings.

Elizabeth waited patiently as the doctor collected his laptop and notes, walking with her down the hallway. Escorting her back to the small but neatly decorated reception area, he turned to smile at his anxious patient.

"We should have the blood test results back shortly, and we will be in touch with you as soon as we do."

"Thank you, Dr. Estrada. I will start drinking more water and keep an eye on how I'm feeling."

"If you start having any pain, please don't hesitate to be in touch with us immediately, okay?"

"I will, thank you."

The doctor nodded his head as he reached out to open the reception door.

Elizabeth gave him a warm smile before making her way from the office to the parking lot. Adjusting her sunglasses to shade her eyes from the sun's glare, she sat for a while in the car. Taking the time to drink plenty of water, she gently rolled up her sleeve as she checked her arm. Poking at the bandage over her vein, Elizabeth contemplated the information the doctor had given her.

"If it's not one thing, it's another!" Elizabeth blurted out angrily as she put the car in reverse to head home.

Not wanting to miss out on her camping trip with Aidan, she promised herself she would get plenty of rest the remainder of the day.

There was no point in lying to her family or keeping secrets, but knowing full well how protective her father and Eloise could be she opted to keep the outcome of the doctor's appointment to herself until the test results were available.

"Just for now," she said aloud as she pulled the car into the driveway and made her way into the house for a quiet evening of rest.

~ * ~

"You won't need your phone Liz, there's no service where we'll be." Aidan pointed to the gadget in her hand as she continued packing her backpack.

Glancing down at the phone, Elizabeth realized he did have a point. Dr. Estrada's office was yet to call back with her test results. Knowing she would be back to the house the following morning, she nodded her head in agreement.

"Yeah, you're right, that would be silly." She laughed as she shut the phone's power off and slid it into her nightstand drawer. "No point in carrying added weight!"

"Exactly!"

Aidan reached for her bag to carry it out to his vehicle. Watching the handsome young man walk down the hallway with her overnight pack, she turned to give Tito a hug and kiss goodbye.

"I'll see you tomorrow morning little one." Elizabeth cupped Tito's head in her hands.

The dog whimpered as he reached one paw up to her open hand.

Making her way to the foyer door, Elizabeth grabbed her waterproof jacket hanging from the closet.

She turned the lock on the inside doorknob as she securely shut it behind her. She had said goodbye to her father and Eloise earlier that morning, knowing they would be keeping themselves busy the next few hours with lunch at Walter's followed by a round of golf. On rare occasions, Mitchell had been known to talk Eloise into joining him on the golf course.

Her father had been sure to use his authoritative voice earlier that day, "Be careful, honey, while you're out tonight."

"Yes, Dad!" Elizabeth had been quick to respond, reading into her father's tone.

It was typical of a father to worry about his daughter, she thought to herself as she smiled at Aidan from the passenger seat.

Reaching his hand over, he gently rubbed the back of her shoulder as she blushed.

After spending so much time with him since their first introduction, she could sense there was a real connection between them. Talking on the phone or texting nearly daily, the two had begun to develop a more intimate bond that went further than just the business of a client hiring an outdoor guide.

"Understand, I am not taking any more payments for planned excursions." Aidan had informed her earnestly during their last phone conversation. "I want us to go out so we can spend some time together if that's okay with you?"

Sensing the reservation in his voice, guessing he was unsure of the reaction he might garner, she had been quick to reassure him that her intentions were the same.

"I like you, Aidan, and I want to spend more time with you too."

"Well, that's a relief! I would feel pretty embarrassed if I were to try and kiss you, only to have you hand me your credit card asking how much you owe me!"

Elizabeth laughed as she had told him she felt like a teenager in school again, which he agreed.

"We're both thirtysomethings, and I don't think we have to feel silly about anything. We are adults!"

Coming back to the present moment, Elizabeth had decided earlier that day that she would tell Aidan about her health issues. It was something she felt she just wanted to get it out in the open.

Hoping there might be a possible relationship with Aidan, it was only fair that he knew what her intimate physical limitations were.

~ * ~

Over the course of the next several hours, Aidan and Elizabeth enjoyed a long and slow leisurely hike into Na Pali. Having promised herself she would take it easy and drink plenty of fluids, she opted to leave her camera gear behind for the overnight hike to carry an extra liter of water instead.

"I do have a small pocket camera with me," Elizabeth said when Aidan noticed she left her equipment behind. "I thought I would pack light today. Otherwise, you would have to foot the gear for me."

"Well, I kindly thank you for thinking of both me and my back," he laughed as he kidded with her. Making their way to an open clearing from the footpath, she smiled as she admired the view.

They had finally arrived at their destination for the evening. A small, secluded beach surrounded by the majestic mountain cliffs fronted by gently lapping waves from the sea. The water sparkled like crystals hidden beneath the surface under the sun's rays. Seagulls kept them amused as they watched the birds hunt for food.

"Now I understand why you told me to bring my bathing suit!"

"Yes, ma'am!"

Aidan smiled as he dropped his gear to the ground and began setting up their tent and a small campfire for the evening.

They had only passed a handful of hikers as they made their way through the rainforest, Elizabeth couldn't help but wonder why there were no other campers at what looked to be such a serene and coveted spot.

"I'm surprised too," Aidan responded as he paused momentarily from his physical labor to survey the desolate beach. "Typically, this place is full of campers. Sometimes they come in by boat just to hang out and take in the sun and scenery."

"I can see why they would like to spend the day here, it's so peaceful."

"Well, maybe they all got my memo to stay off the beach for the evening, so I could just hang with my girl!" Leaning over her small frame, he gave her a soft kiss on her cheek.

Feeling herself flush as he gave her a wink, she turned to set her gear down in the sand.

Wanting to feel useful, she reached down towards the rolled up sleeping bags and unzipped the small tent. Making her way inside, she tried to contain her excitement at the prospect of spending the night alone with Aidan in this intimate setting.

The rest of the afternoon was spent frolicking in the gently rolling waves, as the pair made the most of their afternoon alone. Playfully flirting and sharing the occasional hug or kiss, neither could deny the feelings they were developing for one another.

By nightfall, they enjoyed a relaxing evening by the campfire, eating a light meal packed by Eloise that morning. Making their way into the tent, they cuddled up in their sleeping bags as they enjoyed listening to the steady sound of the waves lapping the beach shore.

Realizing she may have overexerted herself, Elizabeth closed her eyes briefly as she drank from her water jug. Sensing waves of lethargy coming on, she took several deep breaths.

"Are you feeling alright?" Aidan leaned over her shoulder as he looked on with concern.

"Just tired, it's been a long day." Elizabeth smiled as she contemplated telling him about her doctor appointment the day before. Making the sudden decision to just come clean with Aidan, she sat up suddenly and turned to look him directly in the eyes.

"I can't have kids." She found herself suddenly blurting out. Reaching her hand up to rub the scarf she had carefully tied around her hair, she watched him intently for a response.

"Well, if it's any consolation, neither can I," he replied as he smiled at her surprised reaction.

"You're kidding, right?"

"Nope, not kidding!" Aidan continued to smile as he watched her eyes widen with surprise. "Let's just say…the parts inside the equipment, don't function as well as the equipment itself."

Feeling a sense of relief, Elizabeth couldn't help but almost laugh as she blurted out. "I have no parts at all!"

"Imperfections are what make us human." Aidan leaned over and gave his companion a kiss on the forehead.

"How did you find out?" Elizabeth couldn't help but ask, curious to know more.

"Well..." Aidan rolled over onto his stomach as he hoisted himself up slightly on his forearms. "I dated a girl all through college, and when we were in our mid-twenties, we decided to get married. That was long before I came to Hawaii."

Aidan keenly watched Elizabeth's reaction as she gave him a reassuring smile, indicating it was okay to continue.

"We were married for two years, and it became obvious that we weren't able to have children once we started trying. We saw doctors, and it was determined to be an issue on my end. Six months later she was handing me divorce papers."

"Oh, my gosh, really?"

"Yep! She always had it in her mind that she wanted a large family with kids, and I wasn't going to be the one to give her what she wanted."

"I'm sorry, but that seems selfish!"

"Well, I did love her, and I didn't want to keep her from being happy with a family of her own." Aidan smiled as he propped his head on one hand, running his free hand through his disheveled hair.

"Do you still keep in touch?"

"Yeah, we do actually. A few times a year we email to check in and catch up. She's a proud mother of four now, and I couldn't be happier for her."

"That says a lot about your character, that you could be so amicable afterward...and that you're not afraid to talk about it." Elizabeth couldn't help but feel a sense of pride knowing how selfless Aidan was in the pursuit of the happiness of others and his comfort of speaking so openly about it.

"I found no reason to be otherwise. She's a great person and has a good heart. We could have adopted eventually, but I knew for her, it wouldn't have been the same thing. She wanted children of her own, and I understood that. Besides, I don't find there should be a reason to be embarrassed about my not being able to contribute to reproducing offspring. It is what it is, no point in hiding it away from the world if the world wants to know."

Reaching over to stroke his forefinger lightly across Elizabeth's cheek, he gave her a wink. "Okay missy, your turn, what's your backstory?"

She bit lightly on her lower lip as she crossed her arms in front of her, gently resting her head comfortably.

"Well, in a nutshell, I had everything taken out two years ago. My doctors determined I was in a high-risk category for developing the same cancer that killed my mom and we decided preventative maintenance was my only option."

The young woman sighed heavily as the memory of her mother passed through her mind.

"I dealt with depression for years due to the stress of always worrying that I was going to develop the same illness that she suffered. Watching her slowly die, wondering if I was going to go through the same agonizing process."

"I can't imagine how difficult that was for you, having to watch her suffer."

"It was traumatizing. You can hide it from others, on the outside I mean. People think you've healed from the pain and the loss, but they have no idea just how much of that pain you carry inside. There's not a day that goes by that I don't think about my mom and the stress of worrying, for years, that I would get sick as well. It takes its toll on you, mentally and physically. If it wasn't for my dad and Eloise, I don't think I would have ever been able to get this far without completely losing it."

Elizabeth felt the tears swell in her eyes as she looked away from Aidan for a moment, trying not to convey the frustration she was now feeling.

"Everything has been fine for me health-wise the last few years, all my checkups were normal…" she struggled to find the right words as she felt it was only fair to tell him the truth, "until yesterday."

Aidan raised himself up into a sitting position as he looked her with concern in his eyes.

"Liz, are you okay?" There was no denying the urgent concern in his voice.

"On and off I've been feeling abnormally tired at times, and I've had pains on my side. A few times it's made me feel sick enough that I've thrown up." Elizabeth rolled her eyes, as she couldn't hide the frustration she felt mounting inside of her. "I was born with only one kidney and the doctor at the clinic yesterday thinks that I may have developed some complications with the medication that I've been prescribed to take since the surgery."

"Are you feeling okay right now?"

"I'm just tired."

"You know, we shouldn't have done all that hiking today if you weren't feeling good."

Elizabeth rolled over onto her back as she closed her eyes. "I know, I should have told you earlier. I'm sorry. I just…I just wanted to spend time with you."

Turning over to her side, she gazed at him with an earnest look in her eyes. "I want to be truthful with you, that's why I wanted to tell you now."

"Come here." Aidan reached over as he pulled her closer to his side. Wrapping his arms reassuringly around her shoulders, he held her close.

"I want you to get plenty of rest now. We go back first thing in the morning, and then you take it easy at home until the doctor calls, do you hear me?" he whispered as he kissed her lightly on the cheek.

"Yes, I will. I promise!" Letting out a deep and relaxing breath, she closed her eyes as she fell asleep in his arms.

~ * ~

"Elizabeth!" Aidan frantically called out to his companion as her seemingly lifeless body lay next to him. A wave of fear flooded over the young man. "Elizabeth, please, wake up!"

Checking her pulse, he felt panic closing in. It was early dawn, and Elizabeth lay motionless in her sleeping bag.

Completely alone, Aidan tried to stay focused as he scrambled to gather his backpack and radio. Deep within the rainforest with no phone signal, Aidan knew he would have no choice but to carry her over a mile to the next post where he could attempt to get a radio signal from the emergency box. Knowing they were over four hours away from his vehicle, he couldn't take the chance of trying to carry her all the way back. He had to do something now.

Checking Elizabeth's vitals once more, Aidan took a deep breath as he hoisted the unconscious woman into his arms. Pacing himself, he walked as quickly as he could through the dense vegetation surrounding the hiking path. Clambering over loose dirt and rocks, he continued to keep a brisk pace as time was of the essence. He had been left with no alternative but to leave their belongings behind.

"Please get us through this." Aidan prayed as he tried to maintain a steady composure. Never in all his life had he been as terrified as he was at that very moment.

Looking down at the stillness of her body, he fought back tears as he paused briefly to hoist her upper body closer to his chest. Her arms dangled as he tried in vain to keep moving as quickly as he could.

163

Keep going, keep going, a voice repeated over and over in his head as several minutes passed by. He knew full well the worst of his journey was yet to come.

Jogging as best as he could up the clearing of the hillside, Aidan dropped to his knees as he carefully laid Elizabeth down. Noticing a responsive gesture in her body, he knelt over her and saw her eyelids slowly flutter.

"Elizabeth, can you hear me?"

She opened her eyes slowly, trying to speak. A pain-stricken look crossed her face as he tried sitting her up.

"It hurts all over." Unable to hold her head up, she slumped into the cradle of his arms.

"Try to stay awake Elizabeth. I'm going to call for help okay, just stay awake hon."

Aidan gently laid her back down on the soft heather grass as he stumbled to reach for his walkie-talkie. A small radio he always carried in the forest for emergencies.

Taking a deep breath, he scrambled for the phone box as he opened it to find the wires to adapt his radio.

"Please work, oh man, please just work!" he muttered aloud as he frantically tried to reach a radio frequency.

"John, come in John, are you there, we have an emergency!"

Static response continued to emanate from the radio as Aidan quickly looked over his shoulder to check on the sick woman. Running his free hand through his disheveled hair, relief flooded over him as he watched her attempts to stay awake.

"Aidan, this is John, what is your emergency, over."

"John, I need a helicopter to the emergency helipad, mile marker four. Elizabeth is sick, and she is barely responsive. She's going in and out of consciousness."

"Roger that Aidan, I will call emergency response now, be careful buddy."

"Thanks, John. Over and out." Disconnecting the radio, Aidan ran back to Elizabeth as he saw her attempting to lift herself up.

"Don't try to move, Liz."

"I'm going to be sick," she cried out as she fell to her side.

Grabbing her as quickly as he could, he squatted over her to help hold her up as she began to vomit. Too weak to reach up and wipe her face, she cried out in both pain and embarrassment. Unfazed, he instinctively slid the scarf off her head to wipe the frothy mucus from her mouth.

"Don't be embarrassed Elizabeth, I don't care. You're unwell, and the only thing that matters is getting you out of here."

He continued to hold her head up as he carefully cleaned her face. Brushing her damp hair away from her eyes, he gave her a gentle kiss on the forehead. Adjusting his backpack, he lifted her up again. Balancing himself and his precious load, Aidan blinked several times as a light sprinkle of rain began to fall.

He made his way back down the clearing towards the hiking path. They had passed the point only yesterday, Aidan knew what lay ahead. The only way to reach the helicopter landing area quickly would be to take a shortcut.

"Elizabeth, listen to me, I'm going to have to carry you across the river. There is no safe way of passing around it quickly."

Reaching the riverside, Aidan scanned the river bed. Large, wet boulders barricaded both sides of the river bank.

"I've crossed it many times before. I know the current, but we're both going to get soaked." He glanced down at his companion as she slowly nodded her head.

Aidan tried his best to keep his balance nearly slipping down the rocky embankment. His trekking shoes, covered in mud, held firmly to an area of pebbles close to the riverbed.

Familiar with that exact location, using a large tree stump in the bed of the river as a marker, Aidan knew that was the spot he wanted.

Slowly and carefully entering the water, he hoisted Elizabeth up as high as he could. Taking one calculated step after another, he continued to move deeper and deeper into the water.

He could feel the coldness of the water rushing over them, splashing about their bodies as the current moved swiftly around them. Now waist deep, he continued to move as quickly and cautiously as he could.

"Are you okay?" he asked her as he dredged his way out of the moving current and onto the embankment on the other side.

"Yes. Wet." A weak smile crossed her face as she closed her eyes again.

"Yes, I know, soaked." He attempted to reciprocate her humor as he swiftly hiked over several fallen tree roots and up another crudely-marked trail.

Several minutes passed as Aidan made his way up another hillside to a flat clearing. In the distance, and much to his relief, the faint whooshing sound of a helicopter could be heard approaching.

Within moments a blue and white emergency response unit helicopter was hovering over them.

Holding Elizabeth upright and placing his free hand over her face, Aidan turned his head to shield himself from the flying debris as the helicopter descended onto the helipad.

"She's responsive, but just barely!" Aidan hollered over the noise of the engine and propeller as two paramedics ran to their side. Securing her onto a stretcher, they hoisted her up as they quickly ran back to the aircraft. Wasting no time, the pilot of the helicopter began his ascent back into the air.

Questions continued to race through his mind. Self-doubt also began to creep over him as the aircraft made its way to the hospital.

What had happened, and why?

~ * ~

CHAPTER TWELVE ~ The Harsh Reality

"I don't understand, what's happened to my daughter?" Mitchell rushed into the emergency room as he and Eloise scrambled to make their way down the corridor with the physician waiting for them at the door.

"Mr. Fisher, I'm Dr. Estrada." The doctor extended his hand in Mitchell's direction. "Your daughter was seen by our clinic for the fatigue and pains she had been experiencing the last few weeks."

"Few weeks?" Eloise couldn't help but blurt out as her eyes widened in disbelief.

"Yes." Dr. Estrada nodded his head as he acknowledged Eloise's startled reaction.

"In her defense, she was quite shocked herself. Apparently, the pains had started out barely noticeable. She attributed the discomfort to a residual side effect of the change in her estrogen therapy medication. She didn't think the symptoms were out of the ordinary."

The doctor continued speaking as both Mitchell and Eloise followed him down the hall, past a nurse's station teeming with busy staff. Hospital equipment lined the whitewashed walls as nurses and doctors made their way in and out of patient's rooms.

"It's a rare occurrence, but it's not unheard of for a patient to go into acute renal failure from side effects of long-term hormone therapy medication. In Elizabeth's case, the preliminary tests came back positive. Unfortunately, our office was unable to reach her yesterday morning to give her the results. We had hoped to hear back from her by the end of the day, and we tried to contact your cellular phone as well."

Mitchell slowly closed his eyes and he let out a frustrated sigh.

Shaking his head back and forth, he rolled his eyes up to the ceiling and acknowledged the phone mishap.

"Liz left her phone at the house, she went camping and didn't see the need to take it. She called us from Aidan's phone to let us know she had left hers at home. I went out yesterday afternoon for a round of golf and just turned my phone off altogether. We had no idea this was all going on!"

Mitchell looked at Eloise as she reached out to comfort her friend.

Eloise nodded her head as she agreed with Mitchell.

"I just can't believe this is happening!" She looked at the doctor for some encouraging words. "Is she going to be okay? What can they do for her?"

"Well, I'm going to let the nephrologist, Dr. Emery, discuss the next steps in further detail with you. I don't want to get your hopes up, but in a situation like this, surgery is going to be necessary, and you both will need to prepare yourselves. The waiting list for a transplant is lengthy. Given she only has one kidney, we are pushing to bump her up the list. I won't lie to you...it's going to be tough."

The trio had reached the corridor as they turned to enter a simple room. The sterile environment stood in stark contrast to the refreshingly colorful scrubs worn by the staff.

169

Lying nearly motionless on a hospital bed, Elizabeth stared at the ceiling as a nurse adjusted the ominous equipment near the head of her bed.

Stepping away from the bed to make a brief introduction, the attending physician gave them space as Mitchell and Eloise raced to Elizabeth's bedside.

"Dad, I'm really scared." Elizabeth's eyes welled up with tears as she reached her hand out towards her father, struggling to control the anxiety creeping into her voice.

"Honey, it's going to be okay, don't get yourself worked up." Mitchell tried in vain to find some comforting words for his only daughter as he struggled with the fear of the unknown. He reached out to squeeze her hand.

"Is Tito okay? Oh my gosh, what about Aidan?" Elizabeth's face strained as she thought about her dog and her friend.

"Liz, sweetie, I will call Gwen and ask her to watch Tito, and I will check on Aidan shortly." Mitchell squeezed his daughter's hand lightly, giving her reassurance everything would be okay.

"Baby, listen to your daddy, you hear?" Eloise moved to take the nurse's place. Reaching over to rub her hand across Elizabeth's forehead, she brushed the bangs from her washed-out skin. "You know how worked up you can get when your anxiety starts acting up. Try and take deep breaths, the doctors are here to help."

Another nurse, entering the room with a tray containing vials and needles, carefully made her way to Elizabeth's bedside as Mitchell and Eloise backed away.

"If I could speak to you both, please." Dr. Emery motioned his hand to the hospital room door as they followed obediently to a small, empty waiting area. Dr. Estrada, bringing up the rear, also accompanied the group as Mitchell and Eloise warily listened to the prognosis.

The harsh reality was sinking in. Without an immediate kidney transplant, Elizabeth was in imminent danger of succumbing to renal failure.

Eloise covered her face with a tissue as she clung to Mitchell's outstretched arm.

"Surprisingly, your daughter has a high tolerance level for the pain. What we would normally see in patients suffering symptoms of acute renal disease, very debilitating symptoms in initial stages, your daughter's body wasn't displaying. So, it's not surprising to know she didn't immediately rush to see a doctor. She simply wasn't aware the detrimental impact the medication's side effects were having on her body."

Dr. Emery stared solemnly at both Mitchell and Eloise as they attempted to absorb the information. "We have seen in case studies that some female patients, having undergone a hysterectomy with a bilateral oophorectomy and being treated with estrogen replacement therapy, in very small and rare circumstances develop conditions ranging from heart disease to renal dysfunction."

171

"Oh, my goodness, all this just from her medication?" Eloise tilted her head to one side, fear creeping into her voice as she processed what was happening.

"For obvious reasons, we don't want to scare patients out of having necessary surgeries that would otherwise save their lives, especially potential cancer patients. Like any risk, however, there are small percentages that do suffer severe, adverse reactions to long-term medicating."

"My daughter healed so quickly from the surgeries I'm just in shock to hear this." Mitchell's facial expression was strained as he tried to comprehend the diagnosis.

Staring off into the distance, Eloise, seemingly deep in thought, turned abruptly in the direction of the doctors as she stared firmly at them both.

"I will give her one of mine." Eloise didn't flinch as she spoke up unexpectedly.

Taken by surprise, Mitchell turned to his companion as she confidently held her head high.

Eloise turned to look inquisitively at Mitchell. "Do you remember back when she was in high school, we all donated blood through the community blood drive?"

"Yes, I remember."

"When we received our donor cards in the mail. We joked about how she and I could donate to each other because we had the same blood type, but you couldn't because you're B positive."

Eloise continued to look at Mitchell as she calmly explained herself.

Slightly dumbfounded, Mitchell leaned back as he absorbed the information Eloise was giving them.

"You're O negative?"

"Yes."

"You never told me this."

"I suppose it never came up in conversation." Eloise shrugged her shoulders as she turned her attention to the two doctors who were now exchanging glances with one other.

"Well, time is of the essence here." Dr. Emery quickly interrupted the pair. "We typically look at living related donors first, but if we determine there isn't a match, we will go to the first non-related donor that passes the serum crossmatch and antigen testing."

"She's right, I can't donate to my daughter," Mitchell spoke up, already knowing the answer.

"I'm afraid not Mr. Fisher."

Eloise, determined to take control of the situation, patted Mitchell reassuringly on the arm. "I'm not going to let anything happen to our girl, Mitchell!"

"Well, if you are willing and prepared Ms. Johnson, we will get you admitted to the hospital now for testing. If you're a crossmatch, we will want to move forward quickly with surgery."

The group rose as they spent a few more moments in the conversation.

Mitchell watched in admiration as Eloise accompanied Dr. Estrada to the nurses' station. Following Dr. Emery back to

Elizabeth's room, he took a seat in an empty chair next to his daughter's bed.

Not wanting to disturb his daughter's now restful sleep, Mitchell sat for several moments in the stillness of the room. Listening to the periodic beep emanating from the various machines attached to Elizabeth's body, the father looked imploringly at his only child. For all the agony he had felt while he watched his beloved wife slowly die, he was ill-prepared to watch this potential fate unfold for his daughter.

He was slightly startled by the entry of a nurse, who leaned down and spoke to him quietly.

"The man that came in with your daughter this morning, he's asking about her condition. Would you like one of us to speak with him?"

"Aidan!" Mitchell stood up immediately as he realized the poor young man was still sitting in the emergency waiting room.

"No...no it's okay, I will go down and talk to him."

The nurse nodded her head as she smiled. She turned her attention to Elizabeth as Mitchell slipped out of the room and made his way to the closest elevator.

~ * ~

"I am so sorry, Mitchell!" Tears began to swell as Aidan scratched his head in frustration, shuffling his feet back and forth. Unable to control his feelings, he crouched down to the floor as he covered his face with two shaking hands.

"Son, this wasn't your fault." Mitchell leaned forward, attempting to comfort the visibly distraught young man.

"Aidan, listen to me. The two of you would have never seen this coming. It was a rare side effect of her medications that had a detrimental impact on her body. It was only a matter of time before this may have happened. We are all in shock."

Aidan attempted to stand up again, leaning back against the wall in the corner where he had been standing for several minutes.

"Son, I know how much you care about my daughter. I will be eternally grateful to you for doing what you had to do to get her out of the campsite."

"This is the harsh reality now Aidan...Liz is going to need surgery to survive, and all we can do is wait to see if Eloise is a match." The father whispered as he reached out to embrace the young man who had begun to give his heart so freely.

"Is there anyone who can come pick you up?"

"I called Walter. He wanted to come down and check on everyone. Can I see her?"

"Well, she's asleep right now, but I can check with the nurses and when she wakes up, if she's okay with it, then I'm fine with that." Mitchell patted Aidan on the shoulder, still concerned the impact the situation had taken on him.

Looking up suddenly at the sound of a familiar voice, Aidan felt relieved to see Walter quickly heading in their direction.

Approaching the pair, Walter reached out his hand in condolence to Mitchell as he wrapped his arm around Aidan in a fatherly manner.

"How's she doing?"

"She's stable for now." Mitchell glanced down at the floor as evidence of his emotions couldn't be hidden in the pained expression that crept across his face. "She is going to need a kidney transplant, and we think Eloise may be a match, they're running the tests now."

"I know this has been quite a shock to you all." Walter couldn't help but express his concern as he watched Aidan continue to pace back and forth.

"I was going to go back up and check on both the girls. I could let Elle know you're here."

"Would you please, I'd like to visit with Elizabeth for a few moments also, if I may."

Noticing that the minister held a leather-bound book discretely in his hand, Mitchell nodded in approval.

"I told Aidan that once she's awake and if it's okay with her and the hospital staff that he could check in on her."

Turning to Aidan, Walter gave the young man a firm hug.

"Son, why don't you and I go take a walk for a few moments and get some air while Mitchell heads back upstairs."

Just then, Mitchell felt the vibration of his phone in his pocket. Glancing at the screen, he recognized the number immediately.

Walter piped up as he led Aidan down the hall towards the cafeteria for a cup of coffee.

"That's probably Gwen. I hope you don't mind, I called her on my way over."

Mitchell nodded as he answered the call.

"Please, tell me, is there is anything I can do to help?" A concerned yet eloquent voice could be heard on the receiving end. "Do you need me to take Tito for you?"

"Yes, I would be very appreciative if you could. We're all just trying to keep it together right now, Gwen..." Mitchell paused as he forced himself not to get choked up. "I will have to head back to the house shortly to get the girls some belongings, could I drop him off at your house on my way back?"

"Mitchell, please, by all means, anything I can do. Please let Elizabeth know I am thinking about her."

They spoke for a few more moments, and arrangements were made as Mitchell hung up the phone.

Finding himself momentarily alone in the quiet hallway, Mitchell caught himself staring at his reflection in the brightly polished white tiles that made up the hospital wall.

Realizing he was still in a state of shock from the rapidly evolving situation at hand, a reoccurring thought played over and over in Mitchell's mind like a broken record.

How could this all be possibly happening?

~ * ~

"Can I ask you a question, Walter?" Aidan turned his attention from the coffee cup he had been fixating on for several minutes to look at his companion.

"You're welcome to ask me anything. I'm an open book, and you know that." Walter winked as he tried to encourage the young man to uplift his melancholy spirit.

177

"How did you ever get over...I mean, when your wife passed, how did you handle it?"

"You never get over it." Walter smiled somberly as he dutifully answered the question. "You learn to adapt and move forward with your life, but you never get over it. It's a feeling that stays with you for the rest of your days I suppose."

Walter lowered himself slightly forward as he propped his forearms on his knees, coffee still in hand.

"It's that autopilot mechanism that keeps you going after the loss. That clouded haze you force yourself to go through day after day as a means of survival while you're processing the feelings. Eventually, that cloud you felt trapped in that seemingly never wanted to leave, will slowly begin to dissipate. Then, you start feeling a bit more alive again as time passes."

"I don't want to have negative thoughts in my head, but what if, you know, what if Eloise isn't a match." Aidan looked at Walter, the heightened sense of frustration creeping back across his face. "She could die. I care about her so much...I just can't believe this is happening."

"There will be days when you will feel life itself is your worst enemy. You will ask why over and over. You will be angry, frustrated, and feel utterly alone with your thoughts and sadness."

Squinting his eyes from the rays of the sun that had begun to shine through the lightly swaying trees, Walter sat upright as he gently patted Aidan's shoulders.

"Just remember, each day you start to feel that sense of desperation creeping up on you, remember you are never alone.

Every being around you have suffered a loss of a loved one. Never be afraid to reach out for comfort and some guiding words."

"I can understand why so many people fear to get close to others. I can't even begin to explain this feeling I have right now, thinking that something really bad could happen, there are just...no words for it." Aidan gripped his chest as he could sense the feeling of anxiety setting in.

"There is a lot of love out there in the world, Aidan, folks just have to be open to bringing that love in a little nearer and dearer to their hearts and minds. Fear is just a natural part of the process."

Aidan forced a smile as he leaned back against the garden bench.

"They ever tell you, you sure are wise for an old man?"

"I've had many years to perfect it! One day you will be sitting on my end of this conversation giving someone else in need some heartfelt, guiding words."

"I sure hope I have your confidence when I'm your age."

"Well, you may not be as handsome as this old buck, but you will most certainly have the life experience to help others!"

Walter grinned at his joke as both men stood up and slowly began to make their way towards the hospital doors.

Wrapping his arm around Aidan's shoulder, Walter held the door as he guided them both back inside.

Standing patiently next to the elevator, Walter leaned forward as he whispered, "You already have the wisdom, along with a heart full of love to give. You always have, and you always will."

"Thanks, Walter, I needed that."

"I know you did, son. Anytime, that's what I'm here for."

~ * ~

Reaching the upstairs floor, Walter and Aidan wandered towards the nurses' station. Getting permission to go down the hall to Elizabeth's room, the pair anxiously made their way.

Sitting close to her bedside, both Eloise and Mitchell were eagerly engaged in conversation with the patient.

"Aidan!" Elizabeth called out as her eyes grew bright.

Standing up from her chair, Eloise gave Aidan and Walter a heartfelt smile as she made room for Aidan to sit closer to Elizabeth.

Noticing Eloise was wearing a hospital gown, Walter wasted no time in verifying the obvious.

"You're a match?"

"I sure am. Surgery in the morning!"

Taken by surprise, Aidan reached over to clutch Elizabeth's hand. Feeling a wave of relief rush over his body, he couldn't contain his excitement.

"Really? I mean…oh my God, I don't even know what to say!" Aidan quickly remembered he was in the presence of a minister. Biting his lower lip, he quickly looked in Walter's direction, "Sorry, Walter."

"No need to apologize, the man upstairs is just as overjoyed as you are." Walter winked back.

"They have another specialist flying in from Honolulu tonight. He's in surgery today, but thankfully he was able to clear his schedule and be on a flight this evening." Mitchell couldn't contain his happiness.

Reaching over the hospital bed, he lovingly squeezed his daughter's legs as he stood up to join Walter and Eloise.

Looking coyly over her shoulder, Eloise smiled fondly at the young couple as they engaged in conversation, now oblivious to the others in the room.

"I say we let these two lovebirds have some time alone," Eloise whispered as she steered the two men towards the door.

"Honey, we'll be back in a few minutes okay?" Mitchell called out over his shoulder as he headed into the hallway.

"Okay, Dad." Elizabeth looked momentarily at her father as she nodded her head, giving him a slight wave.

Realizing Eloise and Walter needed some private time themselves, Mitchell found it was the perfect time to head back to the house for his errands.

"I do believe I have a couple of overnight bags to gather and one furry friend in need of relieving himself outdoors." Mitchell walked towards the elevator as he graciously excused himself from the pair.

"You have my list, Mitchell?"

Patting his shirt pocket, Mitchell nodded his head. "I do indeed!"

"Hug good old Tito for me." Eloise waved over her shoulder as she followed Walter in the direction of the hospital chapel.

Turning slightly as they rounded the corner of the hallway corridor, she watched as Mitchell made his way into the elevator. There was no mistaking the sense of relief and joy that had taken over his face.

Walter glanced down at the woman, keenly observing her behavior.

"You are doing an amazing and wonderful thing for this family. You know that don't you?" Walter offered an extended arm to Eloise as she graciously accepted it.

Making their way quietly into the small room, they took a seat nearest the pulpit. A spread of fragrant flowers and a large, ornate stained-glass window allowed for an array of colors to permeate the whitewashed room.

Finding themselves alone, Eloise removed her hand from Walter's arm as she vainly tried to smooth down her hospital-issued gown.

"They sure don't make these things flattering or comfortable, do they?" She laughed as she tried to readjust one of the ties behind her neck.

Reaching over, Walter instinctively adjusted the garment strings for his companion.

She waited a few moments to answer his statement, then looked at Walter as he finished adjusting her gown tie.

"I'm doing an amazing and wonderful thing for *my* family." Eloise was sure to add emphasis in her response as she smiled up at him.

"I love that girl like she's my own. I have since the moment I met her. I made a promise to her mother that I would be here to take care of her and I aim to keep that promise."

Walter watched with admiration as Eloise sat upright, turning her attention to a large cross fixed to the pulpit.

"I've been there for years to take care of them, and they've been there to take care of me. There was never any dissimulation in our household. We have always been open and honest with our feelings. I know they are just as grateful to have me in their lives as I have been to have them in mine."

Pivoting herself slightly in Walter's direction, Eloise looked to find the right words to continue her train of thought. Consciously rubbing her wedding ring, her eyes made contact with his.

"I haven't been entirely straightforward with you in some of our conversations."

Walter leaned back in his chair as he patiently let her continue.

"We've talked in some detail about losing our spouses." Eloise took a huge breath as she looked back at the cross on the pulpit. "I also lost my baby girl in that car accident, not just my husband. I just wasn't ready to talk about it until now. I hope you understand?"

Walter leaned forward, taking Eloise's hand in his. Encouraged to finish, she clutched his hand with confidence and knew it was okay to let her feelings out.

"I should have died with them, I told myself over and over. Day after day, the pain and sorrow I felt of not just losing the man I cared so much about, but losing my child as well."

Tears began to flow. Walter quickly searched his pockets for a handkerchief as Eloise wiped her face with her fingers. He handed her a small white cloth, and she obligingly took it.

"That little body, just lying in that box. So still, so quiet. Knowing her eyes were never going to open again and look at me with that love and life they were so full of..."

Eloise paused as she shook her head from side to side. "Nothing, not a damn thing on this Earth prepares you for that moment. That moment you have to say goodbye to your own flesh and blood."

Eloise began to sob as the flood of emotion became overwhelming. Walter wrapped his arms tightly around her shoulders.

"It's okay Elle, let it out. Let Him know how you feel. He's here to hear your voice." Rocking her slightly, he allowed the woman the release she needed.

Standing up, she made her way to the pulpit, raising her arms above her head.

"Lord, give me the strength, give me the strength and guidance I need to do what I have to do. *I am here to do what I was meant to do!*" Eloise shouted as she continued to wave her arms in the air. Feeling her heart beat heavy within her chest, she closed her eyes as she felt another wave of emotion flood her body.

"I lost one baby girl, Lord, I don't aim to lose another! Oh no, sir, I will not lose another. You can take me, I am ready…I have *always* been ready!"

After several moments, Eloise lowered her arms. Feeling a sudden sense of peace, she folded her hands over her heart.

Quietly approaching the pulpit, Walter rested a hand on Eloise's shoulder. Feeling a sense of relief and comfort, she instinctively turned and hugged the man.

Standing motionless, locked in an intimate embrace, it was evident to both that they had feelings for one another.

"Let's get you back upstairs, my dear. You are going to need your rest." Walter gently guided the tired woman towards the door.

"How much rest do you think I'm gonna get in a hospital bed?" Eloise quipped as she locked arms with her companion as they made their way towards the elevator. "The only thing that would put anyone to sleep is this hideously boring outfit!"

She pinched the front of her plain blue gown as they entered the elevator.

"Perhaps, but it certainly offers a lovely view from here!" Walter's eyes lit up as he pretended to lean back and look at Eloise's backside.

Her eyes grew wide in horror as she grabbed the back of the gown. Relieved that her backside was, in fact, still fully covered, she realized he had been joking with her.

"Shame on you!" She blushed as she flicked his arm in a teasing manner.

Pretending to glance again behind her back, he smiled flirtatiously, "I know…shame on me!"

~ * ~

It was late afternoon when Aidan was encouraged by Walter to go home and get some rest. Reluctant to leave, he gave Elizabeth a kiss goodnight. Bidding farewell to Eloise, Walter graciously kissed her hand as he accompanied the young man from the room.

Feeling the love in the air, Eloise beamed as she turned her attention to Elizabeth. Sitting upright in her bed, there was no denying the smitten and adoring look consuming her previously frail face.

Making her way to the bedside, Eloise motioned for Elizabeth to move over slightly.

Teetering precariously close to the edge, they both laughed as the older woman struggled to keep herself from falling out of the bed.

"Where are those silly bed rails when you need one!" She continued to laugh as she leaned over the side as though she were searching for something, all the while trying to keep her balance.

"Will you read me one of your bedtime stories?" Elizabeth whispered as she turned her body slightly, taking care not to accidentally detach one of the numerous tubes inserted into various parts of her body.

Eloise opened her bag and reached in retrieving a small bible, a book she carried with her always, especially in her times of need.

186

"Which one would you like me to read?"

"You choose."

Eloise delicately turned the pages until she found the scripture she wanted.

For several minutes, Eloise read from her book as Elizabeth quietly listened. She had just turned the last page when she heard a slight sobbing noise.

"What's wrong baby girl?"

"I'm scared, Elle. What if it doesn't work?" she whispered as she clutched Eloise by the hand.

"Now don't you go bringing any negative thoughts into your mind, do you hear me? Ain't nothing but positive healing that's going to be the outcome of this surgery young lady. So, you just stop your fretting and get that anxiety out of your mind!"

"I could never imagine my life without you in it," Elizabeth whispered.

Eloise gently wrapped her arm around Elizabeth's body as she lightly rocked her back and forth. "You were just a little girl who lost her mama, and I was a mama who lost her little girl."

Pushing Elizabeth's bangs back from her tear-soaked face, Eloise continued to coddle the scared young woman.

"We needed each other, you and me. We needed to be a family, and we became one. You will always be my baby girl, no matter what, do you hear me?" Eloise spoke firmly as she reassured Elizabeth that everything would be okay. "We're going to get through this, you and me!"

Eloise fought back her own tears as she continued to rock Elizabeth, singing one of her favorite hymns softly. Several moments passed as Eloise became acutely aware of the silence next to her.

Noticing the young woman was soundly asleep, Eloise smiled contently as she gazed towards the ceiling.

"You always knew he had a plan for me, Nana." She continued to stare at the ceiling as she nodded her head, acknowledging to herself what her Nana had meant all those years ago.

Slowly leaning back against a pillow, she smiled as felt a wave of calm pass through her body. Closing her eyes, she continued to whisper aloud.

"You were right Nana…you were right."

~ * ~

CHAPTER THIRTEEN ~ Guardian Spirits

Sitting for a moment on his daughter's bed, Mitchell absently lifted Tito into his lap. Feeling as though he had been hit by a truck, he quickly snapped out of the haze as he felt every muscle in his body ache.

It was the same massive truck that hit him the day he found out his wife was given the diagnosis of terminal cancer. There simply was no preparing for the emotions that overwhelmed him.

Sensing his pain, Tito hoisted himself up on his hind legs as he gently licked Mitchell's cheek.

Reaching up to clear his face, Mitchell stood as he put the dog down on the floor.

"I know buddy, I'm sitting here carrying on while you probably have to go out and pee!" Mitchell tried to make himself feel a bit better by letting out a light chuckle.

Walking towards the patio door leading out into the garden from his daughter's room, Mitchell followed Tito out as he ran across the lawn towards the bushes.

Standing for a moment and letting the fresh air from the ocean breeze permeate his skin, Mitchell took a seat on a stone ledge as he watched Tito sniff around the lawn.

Then, without warning, Mitchell sensed the presence of another being. Peering down into the manicured plants cultivated within the stonework, Mitchell realized he was in fact, not alone.

Sitting in silence staring back at him was the tokay gecko. As the lizard slowly made its way from his dwelling under a shady plant leaf, the creature quietly positioned himself on the edge of the stone wall.

Within moments, two small, beady-eyed heads could be seen poking out from the vegetation.

"So, you're a dad too then, eh?" Mitchell sat amused as he watched the two young geckos slowly creep out from their resting spot and make their way towards the stone ledge.

As though on cue, the reptile let out his signature cackle, acknowledging Mitchell's comment.

"I suppose I owe you an apology."

Mitchell turned himself slightly in the direction of the gecko as he continued to engage in a one-sided conversation.

"I hope you forgive me for, well, you know, smacking you across the face. It was a knee-jerk reaction, what can I say. You find a two-foot lizard crawling all over your head...you sometimes just don't think your actions entirely all the way through."

Mitchell threw his arms up in the air in a wide gesture of 'what can I say' as he nodded his head at his scaly companion.

Again, appearing to respond to Mitchell's apology, the gecko let out a throaty bark as he retreated into the vegetation, his family in tow.

Gathering the Yorkie in his arms, Mitchell made his way back to the house to collect the overnight bags. Feeling satisfied he had everything checked off Eloise's 'must have' list, Mitchell made his way to Gwen's house.

~ * ~

Thirty minutes later, Mitchell found himself in Gwen's company as the pair strolled through the garden towards her outdoor studio.

Taking in the fresh ocean breeze, Mitchell allowed himself the opportunity to decompress from the stress that had taken hold of him all day.

"I have to admit, I noticed the strangest thing while I was outside with Tito back at the house. Do you remember that gecko lizard I told you about, from the fender bender incident?" Mitchell struggled to find the right words as he tried to explain. "It was like, he knew something had happened, and it was almost as if he was there to comfort me in some way."

Gwen smiled as she listened patiently.

"I mean, I know that sounds ridiculous, a lizard trying to comfort me. It's not like we were having a heart to heart over a cup of coffee!"

Sensing Mitchell's embarrassment in attempting to explain the scenario, Gwen shifted the sleeping dog cupped in her arms to one side as she gently patted Mitchell's arm with her free hand.

"I believe he has been there all along to relay a message to you, Mitchell." Gwen sat down on a makeshift bench on the studio's porch as she cast a gaze over the serene, sunset horizon.

"How do you mean?"

"Well, in Hawaiian culture, geckos are considered a guardian spirit. They can communicate with the Gods and are

191

protectors of the home. I believe your tokay lizard had a purpose in his life, to look after you and your family."

"He sure has a funny way of showing it!" Mitchell laughed as he rubbed the bridge of his nose, the unfortunate appendage that found its way into the jaws of one said, guardian spirit!

"Consider his actions as messages, warnings if you must. It was his way of communicating with you the inevitability of what was about to happen." Gwen looked down at the sleeping Yorkie as she slowly stroked his silky fur.

"It's also believed the gecko is a spirit of good luck, so take to heart that he has a purpose in your life and the powers that be in the world brought you two together for a reason."

"I will just have to kindly ask him that he not share his guardian powers in my bedroom again at six in the morning, or from my head in a moving vehicle in the middle of the night!"

The couple laughed as they sat a few more moments in silence, watching the tranquil sky change colors as the sun began to disappear into the ocean's vista.

"Feel free to come over to the house anytime, Mitchell. I think you could benefit from some Thai therapy sessions. It's important that you release your blocked energy, it will help immensely in restoring balance and harmony within."

Gwen placed her fingertips on Mitchell's forehead and heart, gently tapping the locations.

Mitchell nodded his head in agreement. He had to admit she was right, and he needed to release the stress he felt.

"Speaking of a restoring balance and harmony, I best get myself back to the hospital with Eloise's things…or I could see myself on the receiving end of some very unharmonious words!"

Mitchell snickered at the thought of Eloise reprimanding him for being so late with her evening essentials.

A faint owl call could be heard coming from the trees as the pair walked side by side down the stone path. Stopping to hear the various sounds the well-hidden bird was emanating, Mitchell listened in amusement to the animal's audible rhythm.

"It's a Pueo owl," Gwen said as she watched Mitchell's reaction to the bird's calling, "Hawaiians believe the owl represents wisdom."

"Well, he's in the right place then." Mitchell smiled warmly at Gwen as he gave his daughter's dog a rub under the chin.

"Thank you again for taking care of Tito. The doctor's hope that with a successful surgery, the girls will be home in a week. I know a certain young lady who will be happy to see this little guy again!"

"No trouble at all Mitchell. Please keep me informed when they get home so I can stop in to visit."

Mitchell waved as he slowly backed the car from the driveway. Feeling more at peace since his visit with Gwen, he focused on the drive back to the hospital and to the unknown that lay ahead.

~ * ~

"How are they doing Doc?" Mitchell stood up quickly as Dr. Emery made his way into the waiting area. The weary-eyed father rubbed at his unshaven face as he waited anxiously for the prognosis of the surgeries.

Having slept only a few hours each, both Aidan and Walter joined Mitchell that morning, eager to hear how the two women had fared.

"Everything looks good, and we feel that the surgeries were very successful."

The men all let out various sighs of relief as they keenly listened to the physician's feedback.

Noticing the doctor hesitated slightly, Mitchell pressed for more information.

"Elizabeth's doing great. We do have some concerns with Eloise, she was displaying signs of hypertension, and we're going to have to monitor her blood pressure for a few days."

Mitchell glanced over at Walter as he listened to the doctor's diagnosis.

"Is she going to be okay?" Walter asked as the signs of concern for her well-being were made evident through the man's facial expression.

"We expect her to make a full recovery. Whenever a patient complains of a racing heartbeat and any other symptoms of that nature, we like to stay diligent. It's not uncommon for the body to display an acute stress reaction, especially right after surgery."

"Can we see them soon?" Aidan asked as he juggled a cup of coffee in his hands, keen to see Elizabeth as soon as possible.

"As soon as they are moved to a recovery room, we will allow visitors to see them. We will let you all know when you can go up to visit." Dr. Emery gave each man a handshake as he turned to head back to the elevator.

After a few more hours of anxiously pacing the waiting room, they were given the okay to head upstairs for visitation.

"I believe we could open a florist shop between the three of us, what do you think?" Mitchell chuckled as they all stood huddled together waiting for the elevator door to open, bouquets of flowers in hand.

Laughing as they took notice of each other's display, they began to joke about who had the best bouquet.

"The three floral stooges!" Walter quipped as they each took turns entering the elevator.

"Well Walter, since you're heading down to Eloise's room, Aidan and I will go ahead and check in on Elizabeth." Mitchell gave the instructions as they made their way to the hospital's second floor.

Nodding their heads in agreement, the three men departed down the hallway in separate directions.

Knocking on the door gently, Walter slipped quietly into the room as Eloise turned her head. Smiling fondly at the man she reached out as he handed her a vase filled with roses.

"They're gorgeous, thank you!" She leaned forward as she took in the fragrant aroma of the beautiful display.

"Only the best for you, my dear." Walter beamed as he took a seat next to her bed.

"How are you feeling?"

"Oh, the usual for someone who just gave up a vital body organ." She couldn't help but laugh as she tilted her head back

195

then winced from a slight pain. "Whoever said laughter was the best medicine, didn't give up a kidney on the same day!"

"You need to take it easy and get plenty of rest. No hanky-panky for you missy!" Walter wagged his forefinger at her teasingly as he carefully put the flower vase on the side table.

"I have to tell you, Walter. I had the strangest dream this morning." Eloise waited for him to finish rearranging the table as he turned his attention back to her.

"I dreamt I was swimming with sea turtles, trying to find my way to the surface to breathe. It was as though I was drowning and then, they were there." Raising her eyebrows, she shook her head as she tried to make sense of the vision she had experienced.

Listening intently Walter smiled. Taking notice that she was looking down at her hands, he couldn't help but observe that she had not replaced her former wedding ring to her finger.

"Your Aumakua was guiding you back to us. They were watching out you while you were in surgery."

"The Auma-who what?" She struggled to repeat the word as she tried not to laugh again.

"The Aumakua...your guardian spirit. Hawaiian mythology says the Aumakua is our loved ones looking after us from the afterlife, manifesting themselves as animals." Walter spoke confidently, as he took care in his words. "The green sea turtles, or Honu, are excellent navigators. It is believed that they bring good luck, endurance, and long life to those they contact."

Thinking about her deceased husband and daughter, Eloise smiled as she understood the message Walter was relaying to her.

Wanting to remain upbeat, she reached out to poke him in the arm, "So, basically, you're saying my guardian spirit is a big, old sea turtle?"

"Yes, exactly." Walter smiled as he gave her a wink.

"Well, at the rate I'm going, I'll be moving like a sea turtle for a while!" Eloise swayed her body back and forth mimicking a slow-moving turtle.

Spending several more minutes alone talking, they both paused to look up as they heard a light tapping on the door.

"Come on in, Mitchell, join the party!"

Mitchell leaned over the hospital bed as he gave his longtime friend a kiss on the forehead.

"I see someone is already here keeping a good eye on our girl!" Mitchell patted Walter on the back as he continued to stand, observing Eloise as she let out a long sigh. "Just make sure our Elle here doesn't over-exert herself, you're on job duty, Walter!"

Mitchell spent a few moments giving Eloise an update on Elizabeth.

"I have a gut feeling Aidan is going to glue himself to the sleeper sofa in her room for the remainder of the week." Mitchell couldn't help but take notice of the fact that the young man was obviously devoted to his daughter.

"I think you are correct on that observation!" Walter was quick to agree with Mitchell.

"Oh, the joys of new love!" Eloise smiled affectionately. As she gave Walter a coy glance, she felt him give her hand a light squeeze.

After a few more minutes of conversation, the three of them were interrupted by a nurse as she came in to check on Eloise. She let the two men know in a friendly but firm manner that the patient needed her rest, and they each hugged Eloise as they left the room.

"You look like you could use some sleep, Mitchell," Walter said as they made their way together out to the hospital parking lot.

Reaching up nonchalantly to rub his unshaven face, Mitchell nodded his head in agreement. "That, and a good shave and shower are in order, I do believe."

"Go home and get some rest, my friend, they're going to be okay." Walter reached into his pocket to retrieve his keys as they approached his vehicle. Pausing for a moment, he looked up from the car door.

"She's a good woman, Mitchell. I just thought I would let you know how I felt."

"That she is indeed Walter, and this is the happiest I've seen her in years."

Mitchell extended his arm out as he gave the minister a friendly pat on the back. "A good woman is one of the greatest things a man can have in his life and our Eloise, well, she deserves a good man by her side. I think that man is you."

Glancing down at the ground for a moment, Mitchell squinted his eyes as he looked back at Walter. The morning sun shone down brightly from above, a gentle breeze floating through the air.

"I've been very fortunate to have two wonderful ladies in my life. It's time for some others to have the opportunity to feel as blessed as I have."

"Thank you, Mitchell, that means a lot to me. I appreciate it."

Shaking hands, the two men parted ways as Mitchell headed home.

While replaying the events of the last twenty-four hours, Mitchell had come to realize that life was in fact, too short. One minute our loved ones are here by our side. Then, within a blink of an eye or a snap of a finger, in one tragic moment, they could be gone.

Reaching up to rub his lightly scarred nose, Mitchell couldn't help but shake his head as he thought about what Gwen had told him.

Everything happens in life for a reason, whether we are ready to accept our fates or not. One thing he felt sure he could depend on…was an obscure message from his guardian gecko!

~ * ~

Nearly a week had passed since the surgeries, and Mitchell was ecstatic when he was given the news that both women would be ready for release in another day or so. Having decided to take a break from the hospital trips at the encouragement of Eloise, Mitchell signed up for his driver improvement class.

"Just take the dang class, Mitchell." Eloise gave him a light slap on the arm as he sat next to her bed sharing lunch.

"This is pretty good for hospital food!" He tried to change the subject as they devoured a hearty tray of seafood and vegetables.

"Did you even hear a word I said?" Eloise pressed again as she rolled her eyes.

"Yes, I heard every word," Mitchell groaned. The thought of having to take a driver's improvement course at his age wasn't exactly something he felt compelled to get excited over.

"Mitchell Fisher, you have been getting on my everlasting nerves for days. The doctors said I would be fine and going home soon. Stop fretting over me and go do something to take your mind off it!" Eloise looked insistent as Mitchell pursed his lips together.

"I pine only because I care."

"I know that." Eloise tried to change her tone as she saw the hurt look on his face. "We have been through a lot this week, we're all tired and just trying to recover and get back to our old selves. Liz is going to be fine now, and so am I, so stop fretting. She's going home tomorrow, and I'll be there just as soon as they sign off on the dotted line."

Mitchell nodded his head as he concentrated on his dessert.

"So, are the two lovebirds officially inseparable?" Eloise asked as she took a bite of her salmon dinner.

"Apparently, I have been passed over as chauffeur home tomorrow."

"The hot Irishman showed you up then, eh?"

"He did indeed. She kindly informed me that as much as she loved me, Aidan insisted on driving her home."

"He's gonna camp out on our lawn, isn't he?" Eloise laughed at the thought of it.

"I'm pretty sure I saw a tent and sleeping bag in the back of his truck."

The pair couldn't help but laugh as they finished their meal together.

"Driver Improvement, who would have ever thought." Mitchell shook his head at the idea of having to listen to someone give him instructions on how to drive.

~ * ~

Mitchell waited in front of the Kapalei motor driving school as he checked the time on his watch. Eight o'clock sharp, he thought to himself as he paced back and forth nervously.

The online website stated that the day-long class would begin at dawn and end by late afternoon. Mitchell came prepared with a notepad as he knew he would be required to take a written and driving skills test by day's end.

Unfamiliar with who the instructor was going to be, Mitchell watched curiously as a dark sedan with tinted windows pulled into the parking lot.

Squinting his eyes from the early morning rays, Mitchell tried not to show an obvious sign of shock.

Stepping out of his car and casually sliding his sunglasses to the top of his head, an all-too-familiar figure advanced towards Mitchell.

"Well, Fisher, I see you took my advice." Kahele gave an almost sarcastic smile as he approached the building's entrance.

"Let's just say, I had some time to kill and thought your suggestion made sense. No point in my insurance skyrocketing over a minor incident."

Mitchell followed dutifully as Kahele instructed him to sign into their log book. Informing his pupil he would be doing his driving skills test first as the forecast was calling for rain later in the day, Kahele collected the keys to the school-issued vehicle.

"So, you like teaching us degenerates how to drive properly, eh?" Mitchell joked as he followed the man into the parking lot.

"Let's just say, I take immense pride in keeping our streets safe from problematic drivers," Kahele retorted as he unlocked the vehicle, "Oh, and before you go asking, it's Instructor Kahele, got it?"

Gathering his nerves, Mitchell sucked in a huge breath of air as he buckled his seatbelt. Putting the car in gear, he slowly meandered out of the parking lot, making sure he took extra effort in watching traffic. Finding himself gripping the wheel, and his knuckles turning white, Mitchell continued to try and stay focused on the road.

Directing Mitchell into a busy resort, Kahele gave him instruction to parallel park in front of the building. Finding the spot precariously narrow, Mitchell turned his head as he began to object.

"It looks…compact." Mitchell tried to find the right words to describe the space he was expected to park in.

Annoyed, Kahele turned his head to look over his shoulder.

"It's fine. I see no reason you can't pull into this spot."

"No, really, it looks too narrow." Mitchell continued to object.

Letting out a frustrated sigh, the brooding man opening his passenger door and peered out over the curb.

"You're fine, just pull into the spot. You do want to pass this exam, don't you?"

"Why do I feel like a sixteen-year-old being reprimanded by his teacher?"

"Because you are in fact a sixty-five-year-old being reprimanded by his teacher!" Kahele shot back.

Feeling flustered, Mitchell began to maneuver the large sedan into the parking spot. Peering over his glasses into the mirrors and out the back windows, he stopped several times to pull the car up as he continued to maneuver into the tight spot.

"For the love of God, will you just park it already!" Kahele let out an exasperated sigh as his patience with his student had run thin.

Feeling the heat from the backlash, Mitchell found himself inadvertently stepping on the gas instead of the brake as he ran the back bumper of the school's car into a parked vehicle.

Turning his head slowly, his eyes narrow, Kahele stared at Mitchell for several moments in silence.

"You seriously did not just hit that vehicle!"

"I don't know what to say, I mean, you made me anxious, and I just hit the wrong pedal!"

"You do realize that I have to fail you on your exam."

"Why, I mean, I don't think we need to jump to conclusions." Mitchell hurriedly exited the car as he ran to look at any damage that may have been done to the other vehicle. Climbing back into the driver's seat, the man continued to plead his case.

"There's no damage, seriously, you can check for yourself." Mitchell motioned his arms in the air as he pointed out the back window. "I mean look at it, it's a golf cart for crying out loud."

"I can't pass you for hitting another parked vehicle, Fisher." Kahele continued to look sternly at the man sitting helplessly in the driver's seat.

Then, as though a bottle had been shaken, all the emotions from the week took its toll. Without any warning at all, Mitchell found himself wailing aloud as he babbled incoherently for several moments.

Startled by Mitchell's sudden outburst, the instructor sat motionlessly.

"Do you need psychiatric assistance of some type? I mean, it's a driver's test. It's not like you're going to lose your license over it. Your insurance rates will not be going down anytime soon I can assure you, but it's not the end of the world."

"I don't need a shrink, I just need…Oh, I don't know what I need. Another vacation from all this stress!" Mitchell began to settle down as he propped his head on one hand.

"Look, I nearly lost my daughter this week. She had to have emergency surgery to save her life, and the only person who could help save her is my best friend. They are both still lying in hospital beds as I speak, and I just haven't dealt with the stress of it very well."

"Obviously not." Kahele nodded his head back and forth as he acknowledged Mitchell's lack of emotional control.

Realizing he sounded harsh, the instructor relaxed his tone as he observed the face of his distraught student. Throwing his clipboard onto the dashboard, he turned his muscular body slightly as he let out a long sigh.

"I'm sorry to hear about your family, Mitchell. I sincerely hope they have a full recovery."

Mitchell searched through his shirt pocket for a handkerchief. Blowing his nose several times, Kahele tried not to laugh as he observed the scene.

"Thank you, I appreciate that. I just feel so responsible."

"How's that?"

"Well, I defiled a sacred space last week, and all hell broke loose after that. I know I never should have thrown that penny!"

Looking confused, the driving instructor rubbed his cleanly shaven chin as he tried to make sense of Mitchell's bizarre statement. "Threw a penny at what?"

"I threw it into Kapahani Falls."

"It's not a wishing well, Fisher."

"I know that! I mean, it was stupid I know. It's a sacred place, and the ancestors are angry. I upset them, and this is my punishment!"

"You know, I could write you a citation for that. Littering is illegal." Kahele couldn't help but be amused at Mitchell's sincerity. "Look, Fisher, you didn't piss off any spiritual beings that are now trying to wreak havoc on your personal life. So just chill."

"Are you sure, because I think I must have pissed a few of them off?"

"Seriously, they are not out to get you. I mean, unless you were, like, greedy or something and wishing for a million dollars. They don't like that sort of thing you know." The man continued to antagonize his student.

"I wished for happiness for my girls."

Slapping his hand to his knee, Kahele pursed his lips together as he watched several tourists meandering around the entryway of the resort.

"Do you want to know the real reason I work four jobs?"

"There's a reason? I mean, I thought you worked all these jobs for the betterment of humanity." Mitchell snickered as he listened intently.

"Ha, ha, a funny man I see."

"Sorry, I couldn't resist."

"Fact is, I have two kids in college, and I'm just trying to make ends meet, so my son and daughter don't have to leave school in debt up to their ears. I have my eighty-year-old parents living with me, so they don't have to go live in a nursing home...talk about zero social life, and I have an ex-wife who left me for a wrestler. A wrestler! I mean, who makes a living doing that? Is that even a real job?" Kahele threw his hands in the air as he shook his head in frustration.

"Wow, and I thought I had problems."

"Everybody's got them, Fisher. None of us are immune, no matter how rich or poor we are. We've all got them."

Mitchell nodded his head solemnly as gave the man a wide grin.

"You know, I have to admit, you have a great smile. Those are some of the nicest teeth I've seen in a long time."

"Okay, that's a little weird." Kahele raised his eyebrow as he looked sternly at Mitchell.

"I didn't mean it like that," he stammered. "I'm a retired dentist. I can't help but notice and admire a good set of chompers when I see them."

"I can let that slide then. Oh, and I suppose I can let your little fender bender slide as well."

"Really?"

"Yes. Go home and take care of your family, Fisher. Oh, and take care of yourself too...get some rest, you obviously need it!"

~ * ~

CHAPTER FOURTEEN ~ A Fond Farewell

Mitchell watched the clock anxiously as he got up from the sofa, pacing back and forth. Overhearing Elizabeth and Aidan talking from the patio outside, he made his way to the sliding glass doors as he observed Aidan affectionately doting on his daughter in the pool.

As happy as Mitchell was to see his daughter making a speedy and full recovery, he couldn't help but focus his concerns on Eloise.

It had been ten days since the surgery. Still awaiting an okay to be discharged, the hospital opted to keep her for an additional few days as they still had concerns with her test readings.

"It's just a little stress and high blood pressure. It is nothing to get all worked up about." She had told him the day before. "The doctors know my family has a history of heart disease."

"Why didn't you tell me your mother died of cardiac arrest during surgery?" Mitchell asked as he watched her intently for a response.

"Because I knew you would be worried."

Mitchell snapped back to the present moment as he felt the vibration of his phone ringing in his pocket.

"Hello?" He answered cautiously, as he recognized the hospital number.

"Mr. Fisher?"

"Yes, this is Mitchell, is everything okay?"

"We need you to come down to the hospital, please," said the voice on the other line.

He hastily ended the call. Grabbing his keys, he rushed to the patio door.

"I've got to go down to the hospital, I will call you shortly." He hollered to his daughter as he made his way to the driveway through the garden entrance.

"Is everything okay, Dad?" Elizabeth asked with concern as she watched her father hurriedly rush to the car.

Not wanting to upset his daughter with the unknown, Mitchell waved out, "I'm sure it's fine honey. I will call you."

Fearing the worst, he tried to concentrate on the road as various scenarios raced through his mind.

What if she had a heart attack like her mother? Mitchell couldn't get rid of the sinking feeling in his gut.

Arriving at the hospital, Mitchell made his way through a side door as he dashed up the stairwell, not wanting to wait on the elevator. Navigating his way down the hallways, he approached the nurse's station.

Noticing there was no available staff at the desk, he decided to head to Eloise's room alone. Finding the door shut, he carefully opened it as he quietly slipped into the room.

Mitchell stood still as he stared at the hospital bed in a state of shock.

The outline of a figure could be seen through the crisp, white sheet pulled over the head of the body. A flood of emotion began to overwhelm Mitchell as he collapsed into a chair against the wall. The room was eerily quiet, as the hospital machines had been turned off and moved back away from the bed.

"I can't believe this is happening!" Mitchell cried out as he sat in anguish, still staring at the lifeless form under the sheets. "I never even got a chance to say goodbye. My best friend, I just can't…" The distraught man couldn't finish his sentence as he covered his face with his hands.

The sheet suddenly flew down as Eloise, one eye opened, stared intently at Mitchell.

"What in God's name are you going on about, Mitchell Fisher?" The exasperated woman hoisted herself up into a sitting position, obviously fully clothed. "Did you forget to take your meds or something?"

"Oh, my gosh, you're alive!"

"I'm sitting here talking to you, aren't I?"

Mitchell stood up as he quickly moved to the side of the hospital bed. "When they called, they told me to come down immediately, well, not exactly those words, but it sounded urgent."

"That's because I told them not to dilly dally and to get you down here ASAP. I just didn't want to be stuck twiddling my thumbs all day!"

"I came into your room and saw all the machines turned off, you were covered with a sheet, and I thought…"

"Oh, for goodness sake, you know how much I hate light in my eyes when I'm trying to rest. I figured I'd take a quick nap while I waited for you to get here. I pulled the sheet over my face to cover my eyes, you goofball!"

Swinging her legs over the side of the bed, she motioned for Mitchell to help her up. He quickly reached over, hoisting her to her feet as Eloise nonchalantly patted down her pantsuit.

Relief flooded over Mitchell as he gave the woman a surprise bear hug.

"You have no idea how terrified I was that we might have lost you."

"Oh, trust me, you won't get rid of me that easily. You'll probably be stuck with me another twenty-five years, Mitchell Carmichael Fisher!" Eloise smirked as she turned to look at her luggage neatly propped in the corner of the room.

"Now be a dear and get my stuff." She pointed in the direction of her belongings as she stood a moment stretching her back and sides.

"I do know a few good exercises I could teach you to help loosen your muscles," Mitchell responded as he obediently retrieved her bags.

"I've seen your version of a good stretch, and I think I'll pass!" Eloise retorted as she shook her head back and forth.

Mitchell shrugged his shoulders, grinning as they made their way to the door.

Pausing briefly and with honest sincerity, Eloise patted Mitchell on the arm.

"Thank you for caring so much about me, you silly old fart. Now get me the heck out of here!"

~ * ~

Finally returning home, Eloise made herself comfortable as she relaxed on the living room sofa. Taking notice of a camping

211

tent pitched in the backyard she laughed as it dawned on her that she was, in fact, correct in her assumptions.

"So, he did camp out in the backyard?"

Handing her a glass of iced lemon water, Mitchell sat down and joined in with her, laughing about the obvious.

"Oh, Walter will be here shortly Mitchell, he wants to grill out this evening, so we thought everyone might hang around and have dinner with us." Eloise shifted her feet up to the footrest in front of her. "Why don't you call Gwen and invite her over?"

"That sounds like a great idea!" Mitchell got up from his seat as he headed into the kitchen to retrieve his phone.

A few hours later, having strolled through the garden, Eloise and Walter made themselves comfortable on the bench swing. Enjoying the evening breeze, the pair found themselves engaging in joyful conversation as they watched from the overlook of the house the gently lapping waves of the ocean below.

Clearing his throat, Walter turned to look at his companion as she smiled warmly at him.

"We could be here for five weeks or fifty years. Life is a precious gift Eloise, the most honorable thing we can do is give that life the opportunities it deserves."

Walter extended his arms out as he took Eloise's hands within his own.

"Each day could be our last. We need the make the most of it now and never take it for granted."

Reaching into his pocket, Walter pulled out an ornately decorated box adorned with a jeweled sea turtle. Eloise carefully took the gift as she admired the stunning craftsmanship.

"Oh, for heaven's sake, it's beautiful!" Eloise sat still as she admired the gift.

"Open it." Walter leaned forward to whisper in her ear as she looked up at him, seemingly taken by surprise.

Carefully opening the trinket box, Eloise gasped as she covered her mouth. Warm tears began to swell as she forced herself not to cry.

Getting down on one knee, Walter gently removed the stunning diamond ring from its safe keeping.

Clearing his throat, he took her hand in his.

"Eloise Gloria Johnson, would you do me the honor of giving me the most precious gift I could ask for...will you be my wife?"

Eloise waved her hand over her face as she felt overwhelmed with joy.

"Yes, I will marry you, Walter Eugene Kalani!"

Walter hoisted himself up as the two held each other in a loving embrace.

"It's wedding time!" Came a holler from the patio as Mitchell let out several sharp whistles.

Not ones to let a good thing pass them by, Gwen, Elizabeth, and Aidan cheered and clapped their hands.

"You knew about this?" Eloise shook her forefinger at them as she walked back to the house with Walter, hand in hand.

"Guilty as charged!" Elizabeth laughed as she reached out to wrap her arms around Eloise.

"Well, what can I say, he did come to me and ask for your hand in marriage." Mitchell winked as he leaned to kiss Eloise on the cheek.

"And to think, all these weeks I was sure you and Aidan were going to be the ones to get hitched!" Eloise looked down at Elizabeth, her eyes still wide from the surprise.

Looking coyly at Aidan, Elizabeth smiled as she walked back to his side.

Reaching into her pocket, she pulled out a diamond ring.

"We're already engaged," Aidan announced as Elizabeth smiled, putting her ring on.

"WHAT?" Eloise took a step back as she looked completely and utterly shocked.

"We didn't want to take away from your moment. We knew last week Walter was going to propose and we didn't want to spoil that for you. So, we decided to wait to spring the news on you!"

Wrapping her arms around Aidan's waist, Elizabeth looked up at her fiancé as she beamed with pride.

Turning her attention to Mitchell, Eloise looked as though she was ready to say something. He answered before she had a chance even to ask.

"Yes, I knew." Mitchell smiled as he watched his daughter, clearly happy and devoted to the young man by her side.

"We're traveling to Ireland and California on Monday to visit my family. We decided to leave the time frame open for the wedding," Aidan answered.

"Well, then I see no reason why we can't have a double wedding this weekend then!" Eloise surprised everyone as she stepped back to take Walter's hand. "If that's okay with you?"

"The sooner, the better my dear." Walter wrapped a free arm around her shoulder.

Aidan and Elizabeth both grinned as they enthusiastically agreed, a double wedding it would be!

Moving to the middle of the circle, Gwen clapped her hands together. "Well, I just happen to know a lovely little spot right on the water complete with a beautiful garden backdrop!"

The rest of the evening was spent making plans for the celebration at Gwen's property as the kindly woman took complete charge as the wedding planner. Within hours, all the arrangements were made with a florist, caterer, and dress shop in town. Walter called his sons to invite them to join in on the festivities.

"Aidan, dear, were you able to reach your family?" Gwen called out from the dining area as she was coordinating with a friend at a local resort for guest rooms.

"I did, I just got off the phone with my mom. She, my sisters, and my grandparents will schedule a flight in on Friday," Aidan replied from the patio. "My dad can't make it out, but he and his wife want to throw us a celebration party once we're in Ireland."

Elizabeth beamed as she blew him a kiss, blushing when he pretended to catch it and gave her a wink.

Turning to notice Eloise comically watching the two of them, the young woman giggled as she tried to divert her gaze away from Eloise's amusing look. "Yes, I know...we're a couple of loved-up dorks!"

"So, who is going to officiate at the wedding, if our minister's getting married?" Mitchell called out from the patio as both he and Aidan continued to take charge of the grill, making dinner for everyone.

Heading out to the patio with drinks in hand, making sure to stop and kiss Eloise on the cheek, Walter passed the refreshments to the two men. "I have a good friend who insisted on officiating for us. He said he wouldn't miss it for the world!"

~ * ~

It was a gorgeous evening for a wedding as everyone gathered at Gwen's homestead. Close friends and family able to make the last-minute wedding were on hand to join in on the festivities. Making sure everything was perfect, Gwen was a commanding presence both inside and outside of her home as she coordinated the caterers, hula dancers, and flower arrangements. Not to go unnoticed was Tito, wearing an adorable little bowtie around his neck, following his new-found friend as she made her rounds.

Waiting dutifully in the outdoor studio, Walter and Mitchell made last minute adjustments to their attire. Smartly dressed in customary Hawaiian wedding outfits of white linen shirts and khaki colored slacks, both men continued to peer anxiously at the garden as guests took their seats. Tightening the red sash he had tied around his waist, Walter beamed as he adorned his neck with a green maile lei.

Noticing a well-groomed man heading in the direction of the studio, Mitchell laughed aloud as he recognized the stand-in minister immediately.

"So, you're an ordained minister as well are you?"

"Good to see you, Mitchell." Kahele gave him a huge grin as he patted the man on the back. "I am indeed. Just one of the many hats I wear on our fine island!"

"Nice to see you, John, thank you for being here with us today." Walter earnestly shook his friend's hand.

"Wouldn't have missed it for anything buddy!"

"So, now I know your real name!" Mitchell chuckled as he watched the two men engage in brief conversation.

"Today, Mitchell, you can just call me John." Kahele grinned as he turned to head back to the garden. Passing Aidan on the walking path, the men gave each other greetings as the younger man quickly advanced towards the studio.

"Mitchell, you have been summoned to the house. Walter, you and I have been summoned to the garden," Aidan instructed as they all headed in their respective directions.

Back in the house, Elizabeth, having already been fitted into her dress, spent the last few moments helping Eloise get ready. Lightly pinning a delicate lei around Eloise's hair, the young woman hugged her as she continued to put the finishing touches on the bridal dress.

"Goodness gracious child, who would have ever thought a few short months ago we would all be here getting ready for a wedding!" Eloise gasped as she admired the beautiful and brightly colored lei Elizabeth had draped over her neck.

"Since you put me in charge of deciding on your jewelry, I think I have the perfect choice for you."

"What's that sweet girl, what did you decide on?"

"Something original and unique. Something you could wear any day of the week." Elizabeth reached into her bag as she pulled out a neatly decorated gift box.

Smiling fondly at her, Eloise took the box as she untied the bow. Inside laid a beautiful diamond encrusted heart pendant.

"Oh, for heaven's sake, it's gorgeous honey!"

"Turn it over," Elizabeth instructed as she wrapped her arms around Eloise.

Gently taking it from the box, Eloise held the delicate necklace in her hand as she read the inscription on the back.

"*Forever in your heart, I love you…your baby girl*," Eloise read aloud as she began to choke up with emotion.

"Now don't go crying or you're going to ruin your makeup!"

"I know, I know…I can't help it!" Eloise cried out as she blotted the tears under her eyes.

"I love you, Elle. Thank you for everything you have done for me." Elizabeth hugged the woman tightly as she continued to blot her eyes.

"I love you too, baby."

The teary-eyed women began to laugh as they hastily fixed their makeup. Knocking softly on the door, Mitchell peeked around the corner.

"Are my girls ready?"

"As ready as we'll ever be!" Collecting their bouquets, they followed Mitchell down the hall.

Gathering in an open foyer overlooking the garden, the two women gasped as they admired the scenery.

The garden, ornately decorated with fresh orchids and lit torches, made a beautiful contrast against the violet-blue horizon. The sound of the musician chanting permeated the air while a group of hula dancers gracefully glided around the garden.

Guests turned in their chairs as they observed the wedding party about to make their way down the aisle.

"Just look at that sunset!" Eloise couldn't help but admire the backdrop of the illuminated sky.

"The island's light, Elle, and it's all for us." Elizabeth turned to look at her companion as she smiled serenely.

Mitchell adjusted his lei as he extended his arms to his daughter and longtime friend.

"Will you do me the honor, ladies?"

"We will indeed!" Eloise beamed as she slid her hand through Mitchell's outreached arm.

Guiding the women down the aisle, the trio walked slowly as they nodded and smiled at their guests. Delivering the brides to their grooms, Mitchell dutifully took his seat next to Gwen.

Leaning over, Gwen whispered in Mitchell's ear. "I suppose your lucky gecko was watching out for you and your girls after all."

~ * ~

"Dad, hurry up, we don't want to miss our flight!" Elizabeth called over her shoulder as she adjusted her bag, following Aidan's lead as he juggled their carry-on luggage towards the security line.

"I'm coming!" Mitchell hollered out as he scrambled towards the group. Having overslept that morning, surprisingly, he was the last to arrive at the airport to see the couple off on their whirlwind honeymoon travels.

Joining Eloise and Walter, Mitchell gave the young couple hugs as they all bid farewell. Juggling Tito in his arms, Elizabeth kissed her dog on his forehead as he happily licked her cheek.

"I'll be home soon, little man." She cupped the dog's chin in her hand as she gave him another kiss on his nose.

Heading through security, the couple stopped briefly as they gathered their belongings from the conveyor belt.

"Love you guys!" Elizabeth called out as she spun around to wave to her family.

"We love you too, safe travels!" Mitchell waved back as he watched his daughter and his son-in-law disappear around a corner.

Mitchell turned his attention to Eloise as she stood there, still waving her fingers in the air.

"Missing them that much already are ya, Elle?"

"No, I'm just waving goodbye to my other kidney." Eloise smiled as she gave her friend a coy side glance.

Knowing he would be eternally grateful for the sacrifice she had made for his daughter, Mitchell smiled back at her.

Walter took Eloise's hand as they all made their way towards the exit doors. "Any plans today, Mitchell?"

"Why, yes, I do. I have a lunch date with one very lovely yoga instructor." Mitchell grinned.

Leaning over, he kissed Eloise on the cheek as she patted him on the shoulder.

"You have an amazing wife here Walter, cherish her always!" Mitchell's eyes danced as he fondly watched his friend head in the opposite direction with her new husband.

"I will indeed. I'm a blessed man!"

Stopping for a moment, Eloise turned as she blew a kiss in Mitchell's direction. "Go enjoy that lunch date, Fisher. Oh, and don't do anything I wouldn't do!"

"I think you're one step ahead of me...Mrs. Kalani!"

Wagging her forefinger at him as she mockingly scolded him, he put his hand up in the air giving them both a wave farewell.

Everything happens for a reason, Mitchell thought to himself as he peacefully made his way back to his car. Placing Tito in the passenger seat, Mitchell adjusted his sunglasses as he lowered the convertible's top.

"I believe an extended stay on the island may be in order, what do you think Tito?"

The Yorkie gave a vigorous bark as Mitchell laughed, navigating his way down the highway in the direction of Kapalei.

~ * ~

Made in the USA
Lexington, KY
14 November 2017